Accidental Death

of a Terrorist

Crime Passionnel

In Southern Italy

Sedley Proctor

This book is entirely a work of fiction. The names, characters and incidents portrayed in it are the work of the author's imagination. Any resemblance to actual persons, living or dead, events or locations is entirely coincidental, but completely plausible.

Accidental Death of a Terrorist
First published in Great Britain by
Leopard Publishing Ventures Ltd
Hampshire SO212PR
www.the half days.com

ISBN: 978-0-9574550-7-8

For my Apulian friends who, in darker times, shall continue to bask in the sun.

Contents

Ice, why hollow? - She wrote, from quibble to pun…
And back again. Just for fun.

***

The Watcher's Decree

This is how she remembered it, in hospital, drifting in and out of consciousness, under the influence, it seems, of sister morphine:

As a special treat, after dinner, she was allowed to disturb her grandfather up in his observatory. The telescope was angled through an open window in the roof. Even in summer it was cold, and her grandmother would tell her to put on a coat over her pyjamas.

When he had finished his observations or consulting his charts, her grandfather would ask her to fetch the bottle of sustenance from the medicine chest. With a tumbler in his hand, he began:

"One day, Fe was coming out of the changing rooms of his local baths when he saw Ce standing in the shallow end tucking her long black hair into a white bathing cap.

As Fe came through to the pool, he must have startled Ce. She jumped into the water and swam up to the deep end.

Fe dived in and swam the length of the pool. When he looked up, Ce was down at the shallow end.

They carried on swimming back and forth until a school party came and spoiled everything.

Fe worked in a computer office on the fifty-first floor. Fe wrote poems between bites. These poems, dedicated to the nymph of the pool, the white capped bather and the lithe swimmer, he left in the changing room for Ce. But when Ce did not acknowledge his poems, Fe became depressed and stopped writing. Moping by the pool like a lovesick teen.

Ce came up to him and poked him in the belly:

"Where are your poems, ninny?"

This seemed to break the ice. Fe made up a new poem on the spot called the Speechless Poet and the Dried up Devil of Words.

Soon they were dating. Fe would write his poems: good, bad and indifferent. Ce was moved one way or another, giggling or reduced to tears. They fell head over heels in love.

One day, on the way home from work, Fe was approached by a stooped Italian with plucked eyebrows called Serafino.

Serafino invited Fe to a bar and offered Fe a drink and some olives. "The barman here makes the best spritz in town," he said.

While Fe sipped his spritz, Serafino told him about the watchers' decree.

Fe was confused. "I'm sorry," he said. "I don't get it."

"There is nothing to get," said Serafino. "That is the way it is. You have transgressed the laws in the eyes of the watchers."

"Well," Fe said, "that doesn't seem to be fair…" He and Ce were in love, and nothing was going to stop their love.

Serafino was adamant; the watchers had decreed. Fe suddenly felt indignant. If there was sin or transgression in this, they did not know it. For how could they know they were transgressing laws when all felt natural to them?

Since they were not Catholic, or even religious, Fe and Ce got married in a registry office. They invited all their friends to the party afterwards in Fe's office on the fifty-first floor. Fe's boss made an unfunny speech; Fe riffed on the wedding party and his new wife and his boss's unfunny speech. They popped open the champagne and handed round the cupcakes. Needing to relieve himself, Fe made his excuses and went to the bathroom.

In the mirror above the washbasin, while inspecting his teeth, Fe thought he caught sight of a stooped figure. Was it Serafino? What was he doing in the bathroom on the fifty-first floor? But there was no time to speculate. Fe was needed to hand round more cupcakes and he soon forgot all about it.

Moved by all the commotion and good cheer, Fe made up a poem in rhyming couplets on the spot. Everyone clapped. "Bravo, Fe!" His boss declared his poem on the theme of cupcakes, though not technically a speech, a fine addition to the difficult art of matrimonial address.

Fe and Ce went on their honeymoon. They'd put all their savings into going somewhere wild and exotic, most probably Vietnam. Fe riffed on their jungle paradise. They visited great temples with fiery gods and inscrutable Buddhas. They ate spicy food with chopsticks and they took rides in rickshaws and pretended they were colonial tourists.

"It could not be more perfect," declared Fe as they were walking in the long grass.

Ce agreed:

"It could not be more perfect, my love."

Fe stooped to kiss Ce. Ce clung to him to receive his kiss. As she did, she collapsed.

Fe rushed Ce to hospital, but it was too late. Ce had been bitten by one of those poisonous snakes that kill you after a few hours. Ce died in Fe's arms.

Fe flew home and sank into depression. He could only think of that bitter asp that had taken Ce away.

He went to the bar and drank himself silly, though he refused the barman's spritz. He turned up at work two weeks late and fell asleep at his desk. When he woke up, everyone had gone home but for a stooped figure. "Serafino," he cried. "What has happened to Fe? - You must help me find her."

Serafino was moved to pity. "Come on," he said, "we have no time to lose."

They took the lift and travelled from the fifty-first floor down into the underground basement below the underground car-park...

Ce was sitting at a desk with her back to him. Fe called out to her, but she did not see him. He took out a poem and read it to her, but she did not hear it. He called to her:

"My love, hear my singing voice!"

He read the poem again. But Ce was equally deaf to his words. Serafino whispered to him. "Go back to the lift. Go up to your office on the fifty-first floor, but whatever you do, do not look back."

Fe stepped back in the lift. The lift began to ascend. Although he remembered Serafino's words, Fe could not help it. He turned round.

In the room where no one came dreaming of Michelangelo there were four different videos that could be watched from low lying seats covered in felt. As I sat down to watch, I kept looking across at the others and glimpsing, through foliage, a man crawling around in a pig mask. Nonetheless, the bluesman was quite oblivious to it all.

*****

The Devil Doesn't Hear Me

Betty, at 28, was beginning to feel her biological clock. She wanted to leave home and get married. Arturo, on the other hand, had no intention of tying the knot. But this did not deter Betty.

Arturo was damn good looking. He was broad-shouldered and muscular with a slim waist. He had a long, dark, mane of hair and green eyes. If Betty never tired of looking at Arturo, girls, even men stopped in the streets to stare at him. Betty was not vain for herself, but rather flattered for the attention he received. All this would have been easy to accept if it only came down to looks, but Arturo had a difficult – indeed complex personality. People who knew him described him as moody or broody. He was thought of as a private individual, but not unfriendly. Betty wanted desperately to unlock the mystery of his personality, even if she realised this was quite impossible.

In Arturo's apartment block, there lived an old man who she would meet on the stairs, or coming out of the lift. Always immaculately dressed in a suit, and sporting a wide-brimmed hat that reminded her of a brigand, the old man played a curious game. Either, he would blank her or tip his head to hide his eyes under the brim of his hat. If Betty felt the old man was expecting her to make the first move and say "Good morning, sir", he was always too quick to deny the opportunity. Soon she began to be cheerfully irritated by his cunning.

Then, once, in the early summer, when she was driving along the seafront, she saw the old man sitting on the wall talking to some men. In contrast to the times before, he was wearing a pair of faded shorts and a grubby T-shirt. This aspect of his appearance took her quite by surprise, as did his demeanour. The men surrounding him laughed and held onto their beers, while the old man held court. Surrounded thus, he exuded a kind of laddish charisma that belied the dignity of his usual brigand attire.

What was going on? What was the old man about?

Out of some instinct, in those early days of their relationship, Betty had not dared to press Arturo. Certain conversations were off limits. And yet Betty was no fool. The old man's flat was on the floor above Arturo's; they shared the same surname: Moro. Though it was obvious that they were related, they never seemed to speak. The relationship between father and son was non-existent. They conducted their lives, as if indeed they were invisible to each other.

Finally, one day, out of frustration with what she perceived to be his distance and indeed emotional absence, Betty decided to confront Arturo about the old man. An argument ensued - perhaps the first serious argument of their relationship. Arturo reacted with vehemence; it was not a subject he was prepared to discuss; Betty was at first annoyed, then outraged. "What can be wrong with talking about your father?" Arturo told her it was none of her business. Betty accused him of being closeted and emotionally repressed. She threatened to end their relationship. – "How can I trust you if you fail to tell me what is going on here?"

"You have no idea what you are talking about!"

Arturo left the room in an apparent rage. He returned a few minutes later with a large brown manila envelope. "Here," he said, throwing the envelope on the table. "Perhaps this will give you your answer."

"You don't want to read it," he said with bitterness in his voice. "It should be thrown away, consigned to the dustbin of history."

"So, you are saying I mustn't read it then?"

"Mustn't! Shouldn't!"

Arturo threw up his arms.

"I honestly don't know why I kept it, but perhaps now it will serve its purpose."

Arturo did not say anything further; instead, he sat down and switched on the TV.

Hesitating now, as if before a Pandora's Box, Betty pulled the papers out of the brown manila envelope and began to read the words printed in the old man's battered type:

If the Devil doesn't hear me, I hear Him.

There is no world for me outside the walls of Verona, except purgatory, torture and hell itself.

***

The Maid's Tale

The rider came in the middle of the storm. He found them sheltering from the rain in the old trullo at the edge of the olive field that once did belong to her da. As he rang out his clothes, he joked with the lasses:

Who was going to comb his tash?

When the sun came back out, he stripped off his shirt, and helped them pile up the nets. He picked up a sack of olives, tossed it on his back, and took it over to the tractor.

His name was Beppe Moro, and he was the quartermaster on a ship docked down at T. He had broad shoulders and dark skin befitting of the name everyone knew him by - the Moor.

When he came back the following day with a demijohn and some cheese, her uncle said:

"Don't you navy people ever work?"

The Moor chuckled and replied:

"I'm no lazy-bones, sir."

His ship was up for repairs, you see, and they were going to be around till the end of the harvest.

That's how it went. The Moor come back to help them lift the sacks and move the nets. They were glad of his brawn, but they were also glad the rain held off so the olives wouldn't get water-logged before they went into the press.

Everyone was for admiring the Moor's motorbike, the Mach One as he called it. "When will you give us a ride?" they were always saying.

Though he took care to give them all a ride, he took her twice round the field and up the road to the farm. But when he revved the engine and swung her from side to side on the country lane, the Maid said:

"That supposed to impress?"

The Moor laughed and returned:

"I heard all about maids such as thee who break a man's heart."

On the last day of the harvest he brought his accordion, so they could sing the old songs. Among the favourites were "My Little Pansy", "The Shoeless Princess" and "The Maid in the Olive Press". When the party was over, they were all sorry to see him go back to his ship. "I'll be thinking of thee," he said.

True to his word he was; he sent postcards from all over the Med. On the back, he drew a doodle of a girl with pigtails holding a bucket under an olive tree, and he wrote:

"I am still thinking of thee."

One day he even phoned up from the radio room. They were docked on the Bosporus, and he was looking up at the Golden Horn. He'd been to see the Blue Mosque and the Sultan's palace. "What is the Sultan like?" she asked. "Has he got a tash like thee?"

The Moor returned in the spring. He'd sold the Mach One and bought a Five Hundred. The Five Hundred was laden with goodies: cheeses, salamis and special cakes from his village he called "dirty tashes."

"Why is that?" she asked.

"Because when you eat them, you dirty your tash."

"I haven't got a tash."

Laughing, he said:

"I've got something for thee."

"Hast thou?"

He took the ring from his pocket and placed it on her middle finger. "Now you are mine," he said.

"Though I love thee," she said, "I do not belong to thee."

They were married in the village church. The Moor did not skimp on the party. There were more of those cheeses, salamis and "dirty tashes". He got out his accordion and they sang the old songs again, "Maid in the Olive Press", "The Shoeless Princess" and "My Little Pansy".

After that, they went to live in the castle, and that would have been it. Quite a fairy tale! The Moor had been put in charge of the arsenal, you see.

What an arsenal it turned out to be! There was a stack of Lee Enfields left by the British. Some grenades confiscated from the Jerrys; sandbags and barbed wire rusting under canvas; tar and paints; old moth-eaten bedding and uniforms; rotting bunks and chairs, and a powder room full of sand that blew in with the mistral.

The castle was over the far side of the bay from the town. From the parapet, you could see the cranes in the port and the chimneys from the steelworks.

In these conspicuous surrounds, the Moor stripped to the waist and dived off the rocks and picked up sea urchin from the sea floor. He found her hairy crabs in the cracks in the rocks. He even tried to teach her to swim in the moat, but the Maid was afraid of the water. "Moor," she said, "I'm not a fish."

The Moor lost his rag. "What are you going to fetch me?" he said, waving one of those hairy things in her face. "You can't even pick up one of these." But that was all forgot when her auntie and uncle came for a picnic over the holiday weekend.

"Will you sing us a song, love?"

"I will do that just for thee."

They played the old songs again, and the Moor could not have been in a jollier mood when they called for an encore of "Maid in The Olive Press" and "The Shoeless Princess".

The Moor had three friends known by their nicknames - the Cat, the Fox and the Brick A right bunch of jokers they turned to be! The Cat who owned a sweetshop in town wore a pair of horn-rimmed specs but was as blind as a bat. The Fox walked with a limp, an old war wound he said, but everyone knew it was just an excuse when he bunked off work from the Council. The Fox who had many fingers in many pies, was an administrator of a block of flats, which was where the Brick come in; he was the caretaker in the building. Brick by name, brick by nature!

One evening, they'd come round for a hand of cards. All the talk was of the Siren and its Captain that were bringing scrap iron from Turkey. They could not get enough of it, the Siren and its scrap. "Boys, we'll strike a deal with that Captain," declares the Moor. "And sell it up north. I know just the fellows."

"Why, my dear Moor," says the Fox with his accustomed irony, "I can't wait to be introduced to your friends from the north."

"All in good time," says the Moor, chuckling, as he went tripping off down to his cellar for a bottle of fizz.

It was while the Moor was away, she saw it. - The hanky was lying on the floor. She bent to pick it up. Just as she did, the Moor came whistling back into the room.

"Boys, look what I got," he says, placing the bottle of fizz on the table. "Let's drink a toast to Your Captain of the Siren!"

The Brick as you know him can't help it and bursts into a fit of giggles.

"He's going to choke on his tears," says the Cat with his accustomed irony.

"Pull yourself together, man," says the Fox. "Have you no self-control?"

"Indeed," says the Cat, "there be ladies present."

What had possessed her to do it? - To whisk that hanky away in her pocket. Truth be told she didn't think anything of it till the Moor goes looking in his hanky drawer. "What's this doing here?" he says. "I never seen this spotty thing before."

"Get me a clean one," he says. "This is dirty."

This is how it went: The Moor grew sullen. His witty remarks dried up. He would not let her out of his sight. Watching her over his games of solitaire, he would say: "We must clean the old uniforms. Hang out the bedding etc."

Now she was always scrubbing and cleaning. Every day she went up to the parapet with a basket groaning of washing. She began to curse the sight of the steel-works chimneys and the cranes in the port. Would it ever end? – The life of a drudge!

One day, the Moor come home drunk and chases her round the kitchen, crying "I'll have my way with thee!" He grabs her, squeezes her and begins to undo his belt when she picks up the rolling pin from the side and whacks him over the head with it.

Afterwards, she caught the bus back to her village. But it was not a friendly reception.

"Lassie!" her auntie says. "What are you doing here without your husband?"

"The Moor has been very kind to you," she says. "You don't want to upset him."

"But I hates him."

"Lassie," says uncle, "you must put aside your differences and learn to do your duty."

"But I hates him."

Then her uncle takes her aside and reminds her of how things stand with the Moor. In particular, he reminds her of the facts regarding those olive fields, the ones that belonged to her da.

"Lassie," he says, "how do you think we was to pay for your wedding?"

This is how it went. The following day the Moor turned up in the Five Hundred. "You must excuse my appearance," he says, pointing to the bandage under his hat. "I have had an accident, see. Slipped on the stone steps in the castle. Please accept my apologies that I could not accompany my wife." Blah! Blah! Blah! He had brought gifts – a grappa from his cellar and a crate of pineapples courtesy of his friend, the Captain of the Siren. It's just like old times! They sit around singing the old songs: "The Shoeless Princess" and "My Little

Pansy". The whole family plays along with his game. They load the Five Hundred with bread and cheese. Uncle wheels out a fifty-litre can of oil. "With our compliments," he says. "Don't mention it! This year has been a good yield."

This is how it went. The Moor is to attend to business down at the port with the Captain of the Siren and his two associates you know as the Cat and the Fox. He's left the Brick behind with the old shrew, Beretta. This Beretta acts like the grand lady of disinterest. "The Moor is worried about you, dearie," she says over her crotchet. "Don't you think it's time to park your feet?"

"Is work to be done," the Maid returns. "I must attend to the sheets."

"I'd help you, dearie," says the needle worker, "only I got this stitch to finish, haven't I."

This is how it went. She's pulling one of the sheets off the line when the fellow you know as the Brick comes up behind her and grabs her. "Where is my hanky?" he says. "What have you done with it, you thief!"

"Let go of me!" she cries and kicks him in the shins. She runs off. Right up to the top of the castle. She stands on the parapet. She looks across at the cranes in the port and the steelworks chimneys. She looks down into the moat. – She was quite ready (as Old Edgardo said) to jump and take her life.

Of course, if this were a tragic tale, it would end here with the Maid's fall. If it were a sentimental one, her death would chasten the Moor into reform. But it is neither sentimental nor tragic. When the Maid awoke from her fainting fit, she heard voices all around her including that of the Moor. "Well, is it a boy? – Tell me it's a boy!"

The Maid did not move until he had left the room and the old shrew Beretta handed her the baby.

In the field behind the church two peasants were digging a ditch. One of the peasants wanted to have a joke. "Here, boy with no shoes," he cried. The peasant held up the skull. It had no eyes or teeth. The boy with no shoes turned tail and ran all the way home.

***

Boy with No Shoes

For two nights running, he had dreamt about the boy with no shoes. When he woke up, he sat on the edge of the bed, looking down at his feet.

His wife came into the room. "Aren't you up yet? The children are already at school."

"I couldn't sleep," he said.

He put on his slippers and went into the kitchen. His wife poured him a long coffee.

After he had finished his coffee, he went into the bathroom to shave. When he had finished shaving, he went back into the bedroom and put on the shirt his wife had ironed. He got out his suit from the cupboard, dressed and put on his brown shoes. When he was ready, he picked up his hat from the table by the front door.

His wife called from the kitchen.

Yet he did not seem to hear; he was still thinking about the boy with no shoes.

The notary's secretary apologised. The notary did not normally make a habit of being late, but he had been incommoded by a meeting of the Council. The notary he assured them would be with them shortly.

"Baring tractors along the highway!" scoffed one of the women sitting at the long oak table in the notary's office.

She turned to the woman sitting beside her. "You know how it is along that highway," she said, "like passing through the eye of a needle!"

The other woman did not speak, though perhaps there was no need. She was her double in looks and coiffeur. If the similarity between them was striking, it also extended to their *tailleurs*. The only difference was in the broach worn on the collar of one of the twin's jackets. She thought of it as a thoroughbred, but really, as her sister knew, it was a sea lion.

Sitting at opposite ends of the table were their two brothers. Though they both wore dark suits and sported moustaches, there the similarities between them ended, and the differences began. One brother, even when seated, gave the impression of being tall, certainly taller than his sibling, who was a rather stocky individual with a much bushier moustache.

The brother with the thin moustache took out a pipe and a tin of tobacco. He began to prod his pipe with a small metal instrument.

The more exasperated of the twins said:

"Honestly, Antonio, must you smoke that terrible thing. The notary will be here any minute."

She turned to the secretary for confirmation, but the secretary had his nose in the documents before him.

"Well, I for my part can't wait till we get this over."

She turned to her sister who concurred. "It will be a relief," she said.

From time to time, over the next few minutes, the twins would launch questions or make statements. The brother with the pipe would nod or give monosyllabic answers. Neither of the twins appeared to direct a question at their other brother; in fact, they seemed to avoid his gaze altogether. He for his part stared at the brim of his hat that lay resting on the table.

When the notary arrived, the more boisterous of the twins could no longer contain her enthusiasm.

"At long last!" she said. "Now we can get on with it."

The notary, who was a large man with blonde hair turning grey, had some trouble getting round the table to shake hands with everyone. Having introduced himself finally to the less boisterous of the twins, he took the watch from his waistcoat pocket and turned to his secretary who handed him a set of papers.

Noting the time and replacing the watch in his waistcoat, the notary began to read in a clear and practised voice. When he came to the end of a phrase, he seemed to defer to one or other of the brothers, and for good measure to the twins. Though soon, it was apparent, he really deferred to the brother with the thin moustache.

When the notary had finished reading, the more boisterous of the twins said:

"Well, I never... Who would have thought that?"

The notary turned to the brother with the thin moustache. "Now if everyone would care to sign…"

Taking out a silver fountain pen from his inside pocket, he came round the table and placed the document before the brother with the thin moustache.

When he had signed all four papers in the document, the notary took the document over the other side of the table to his brother. "Signor M," he said, "it is your turn to sign."

He placed the document before the brother with the bushy moustache, who took the fountain pen from the notary's hand.

When he had signed all four papers, he picked up his hat off the table and stood up. He walked out of the notary's office without saying a word to his three siblings.

When he got home, his wife and children were already in the kitchen. They called to him from the door, but he didn't seem to hear them. He went straight to the bedroom. He took off his jacket and tie. He took off his shoes and socks. He sat for a moment staring at his shoeless feet. Then he put on his slippers and went into dinner.

At dinner, his family were in a boisterous mood.

They talked over him and around him. "Dad, will you pass the cheese?" His son said.

He ignored his son's question.

"Mum, will you pass the cheese?" His son went on.

His son did something funny and his daughter laughed. "Do that again!" she said. "It makes you look funny."

His son turned round and started rolling his eyes at his sister. "Look," he said. "I'm a zombie!"

He could take it no more. "Will you be quiet," he said.

"I'm a zombie," said his son.

"Quiet, I said." Slamming the table, he got up and left the kitchen.

When his wife came in the bedroom, he was lying on his side. "What's the matter?" she asked.

"I'm sick," he said.

"Well," she said, "I better check your temperature."

A few minutes later, she returned with the thermometer. "Husband," she said, "open your mouth."

He did as he was told.

She put the thermometer under his tongue, and he lay back still thinking upon the crime done to the boy with no shoes.

I feel bad about letting you down and leaving you in the lurch like this. P.S. Let me know if you want anything on the inside. - In Name of the Heel

***

The Watch

Arturo's father had two watches, the one he usually wore on his wrist, and the other he kept in a bowl with loose change up on the commode in his room.

One day, at school, Arturo told the boys in his class his father had given him a watch as a present, but no one believed him. "It's true," he said. "He's got a lot of watches, but one of them he doesn't wear. He said I could have it."

As if to prove it, Arturo described the watches, the one with luminous dial and date, and the other that did not have a luminous dial but still showed the date.

"You're lying," said one of the boys.

"I'm not," he said. "I'm telling tell you my dad's got lots of watches. He doesn't need all of them. He gave one to me."

Arturo's classmate was going to say something else, but just then the teacher came in and they had to sit down to their lessons.

When Arturo got home from school, his mother was in the kitchen, preparing lunch. He put his satchel down in the hall. His mother called to him. "Don't forget to wash your hands."

Instead of washing his hands, Arturo went into his parent's room.

The commode was on the far side of the room. Arturo could not see the top of the commode, so he climbed on the chair next to it. The watch was in its usual place in the bowl of loose change.

Arturo picked up the watch and sat down on the chair to look at it.

He was still looking at the watch when his sister appeared at the door. "What are you doing looking at dad's watch?" she said. "I'll tell mum."

"No, you won't."

"Yes, I will."

Arturo put the watch back and got down from the chair, but it was too late. His sister was already in the kitchen telling on him.

"Arturo was looking at dad's watch."

"You're talking rubbish," he said.

"I saw you," his sister said. "I saw you standing on the chair."

His mother looked at him. "Why were you doing that?"

"I wasn't looking at the watch," he said. "I was looking at the photo of you and papa. Was it taken before I was born?"

His mother looked at him hard. "Well," she said. "Did you remember to wash your hands?"

His sister was gloating and he wanted to hit her, but he had been told not to hit girls.

The following day, at school, Arturo's classmate asked him about his watch.

All day long, he teased Arturo, pointing to his wrist. "Look at my watch," he said. "Go on! Look at it!"

"I have got a watch," Arturo said.

"I don't see it," the boy said. "It must be a figment of your imagination."

Arturo went red with rage, but he could not do anything about it. The boy knew he was lying. Arturo swore he would prove the point and wipe the smile off the boy's face.

That evening, over dinner, Arturo asked to see his father's watch. His father, who was in a good mood, took off his watch and gave it to him.

Covering the watch with his hand so he could see the luminous dial, Arturo said to his father:

"Papa, will you buy me a watch?"

His father, who was tucking into a piece of bread dipped in meat sauce, did not answer. Arturo thought he had not heard him, so he asked again:

"Papa, will you buy me a watch?"

His father put down his bread and reached across the table. Arturo flinched. The blow had caught him on the cheek.

Later, as his mother came to tuck him up, he asked about the watch. "Mum, why can't I have a watch?"

His mother said:

"You must listen to what your father says."

That would have been the end of it, but the following week his father went away. While his mother was busy in the kitchen, Arturo seized his chance and went into his parent's room. He pulled the chair up to the commode, took the watch out of the bowl and pocketed it.

It was the watch with the luminous dial. Arturo realised his father must have been wearing the other watch for a change.

During the night, he put the watch on and stared at the luminous dial under the bedclothes.

In the morning, when he woke, he felt the watch on his wrist. He was still smiling to himself when his sister came into the room. "What are you smiling about?" She said.

"Nothing," he replied.

The watch was on his hand under the bedclothes. "Well," she said. "You better get up or we'll be late for school."

He left the watch under his pillow and went to wash. After he had dressed, he pocketed the watch and picked up his school bag.

Arturo walked into class with the watch on his wrist. He took it off and cupped his hands so his classmates could see the luminous dial. Just then, the boy who had not believed him came up and tried to grab it.

The teacher came into the class; Arturo was shouting:

"Give me back my watch!"

Arturo was in disgrace. His mother came to pick him up from school. Arturo had wanted to explain, but his mother sent him to his room.

Only later, in the evening, did she appear to relent when his sister came to call him to dinner.

While he was eating his vegetables, his mother said:

"Arturo, you must promise me you will never do that again."

Arturo was silent.

"Do you promise?"

"You won't tell papa," he said.

She sighed and looked at him. "Arturo, you must be a good boy, you hear."

Arturo nodded and went to kiss his mother on the cheek.

"Now promise me," she said, "you won't take that watch of dad's."

Arturo's father had returned from his business trip. They sat down to dinner. His mother brought over the first course. Arturo's sister poured wine into his father's glass. She mixed the wine as he liked it with a little sparkling water.

They were all ready to tuck in when his father began to say grace. But Arturo could not wait. – It was home-made macaroni – Arturo's favourite! He picked up his knife and fork.

A hand reached across the table.

SLAP!

Arturo was sent to his room in disgrace.

A few days later, Arturo's father was looking for his watch, but he could not find it. "Where's my watch gone?" he cried. "Has anyone seen it?"

They all started looking for the watch, all except Arturo, that is, who remained sitting in front of the TV.

"Someone has taken it," said his father. "Has anyone been in the flat while I have been away?"

"Beppe," said his mother. "No one has been here. How could anyone steal your watch when we have all been at home? You probably put it somewhere else."

"It's always been in that bowl on the commode."

"Maybe you left it in the office."

"Wife, I am not in the habit of leaving valuables in that den of thieves."

"Have you tried your briefcase?"

"Of course!"

"Your jacket pockets?"

"A hundred times!"

"Well," said his father, finally turning to Arturo, "what about it? Have you seen my watch?"

Arturo shook his head.

His father grabbed him by the arm.

Arturo went kicking and screaming into his room. "If you don't tell me where the watch is," his father said, "I'll give you the worst hiding of your life."

"I swear I haven't got your watch."

What Arturo said was strictly true; he did not have his father's watch. When he had thrown it off the balcony, a man passing in the street had picked the watch up and pocketed it.

All through the worst hiding of his life, Arturo told himself:

"I'm not the thief. He is."

A Story of Chance

"Well," said the young boy. "There is a difference, at least in my mind. Chance is something random. Coincidence, on the other hand, is when we see more than meets the eye."

"What does your aunt think?"

"Auntie thinks I'm splitting hairs. What do you think, papa?"

"I agree with your aunt."

"Because she's much cleverer than you and I?"

"Exactly."

The boy's father leaned over and kissed his son goodnight. He turned off the light and went back to his study to work on the pile of documents from the courthouse.

The prosecutor found he was not in the mood for work. He put his glasses down and picked up his pipe.

As he smoked, he stared at the photo on his desk. He did not see the image the photo invited but rather a series of memories linked to the photo comprising a game of briscolo, a white swimming cap, and a chance encounter on a moonlit night. These images seemed to play in his mind in a timeless puff of smoke.

There was a knock on his study door; it was the boy's aunt, who had come to tell him that she had packed his suitcase.

"I've put in three shirts, an extra tie and some underwear," she said. "I've left the wash-bag on the dresser along with the parcel."

The prosecutor thanked her. He said he was grateful for her presence of mind; he did not know what he would do without her.

"I am going to bed, Panchetta," she said. "Is there anything else I can do?"

"Well," he said, smiling, "I will be off rather early."

"Do you want breakfast?"

"Really, Mimi," he said, "don't trouble yourself."

"It's no trouble."

The prosecutor smiled. The elaborate game of manners played out like a courtship without the erotic charge.

After she had gone, the prosecutor remembered some bills. He sat down, wrote a short note and put a cheque in an envelope before going back to his papers from the courthouse.

The prosecutor's appointments in the capital were all within walking distance of his hotel. He crossed over the river on foot and went to talk to a Monsignor M- in Palazzo "Sisto V". After his chat with Monsignor M-, he crossed back over the river and visited a small office off Piazza Navona for his chat with a little moustachioed fellow who worked for Cisalpine Overseas Ltd. The little moustachioed fellow who worked for Cisalpine Overseas Ltd handed him an envelope, along with several holiday brochures for various islands in the Caribbean, which he secreted away in his briefcase. By mid-afternoon, he had finished all his business and returned to the hotel to freshen up.

A while later, around six o'clock, he dressed for dinner and took the parcel he had brought from home from his suitcase. Then he went out. When he arrived in the restaurant, near the Parliament Buildings, the deputy, who was already seated at the table, got up to greet him.

They exchanged pleasantries.

The prosecutor was tall, but as his nickname suggested, with a little bacon around the middle.

The deputy, who was not tall, looked for a moment with distaste before seizing on the parcel the prosecutor placed on the table.

"How delightful," he declared, "a *minzetta* by the potter Del Monaco."

Putting the box aside, he said:

"I sincerely hope there have been no half measures in oiling the wheels."

The prosecutor smiled at the deputy's joke.

"Parliament," he said, "is always up in arms about something."

The deputy did not comment, but proceeded to the menu.

There was some debate in the deputy's mind about which would be better, the hare or woodcock sauce. In the end he came down on the side of the hare. "The woodcock," he said, "always sticks in the throat."

"On the other hand," said the prosecutor, "you can never be sure to catch the hare."

"I don't agree," said the deputy pointedly. "All it takes is a few good hounds."

If the deputy was known to wags in his party as the soul of DC, the prosecutor was – with some justification – its shadow.

The deputy and the prosecutor went on discussing the state of affairs. None of that, however, concerns us. Since the intrigues of that time have lost their significance, as all intrigues inevitably do, we shall bring things forward to the end of the meal and a stroll down by the river, where we find them again, lingering a moment on the bank across from Castle Gandolfo.

After more intimate and frank exchanges, the deputy walked the prosecutor back to his hotel. They shook hands. "Remember," he said, fixing the significance of their encounter in the newly coined adage, "all it takes is a few good hounds."

It was not late when the prosecutor phoned his son from his bedroom in the hotel. His son was in high spirits; he had done well in a test. "My teacher gave me eight and a half, "he said. "I can't believe it."

The prosecutor was reminded of their conversation of the previous night. "Well," he said. "That cannot be chance you managed to do so well."

"I didn't really study," the boy said. "It was a fluke."

"You mean, chance."

"No, papa, I mean it was a total fluke. It was like I knew what the question was going to be, though I suppose you could call that coincidence."

The prosecutor laughed. "That seems like synchronicity to me," he said.

His son did not understand; the prosecutor attempted to explain. "There was a famous case of a psychiatrist interpreting a dream involving a scarab."

"Papa," said his son. "I don't see what a cockroach has to do with it."

"Not a cockroach. A scarab."

"Well, I didn't dream the question, I just guessed the answer. Because I knew the question, however, I was able to guess the answer."

"You mean you had déjà vu."

"What's that?"

"A special kind of coincidence."

"And not chance?"

The prosecutor laughed.

The boy asked when he was coming home.

The prosecutor promised he would be home soon.

"I miss you, papa."

They said goodnight.

The following day the prosecutor checked out of the hotel and took a taxi to the airport.

Arriving on board the plane, he put his briefcase in the empty seat beside him. He fastened his seat belt and sat back in preparation for the take-off.

The plane climbed out of the low-lying clouds. He saw the Dome of St. Peters and the ancient city stretch out before him in all directions; then the plane tipped and he saw the sea. If for a moment he felt his head precipitating, the plane righted itself and the fasten seat belt sign went off.

The plane was flying in a southerly direction over the Mediterranean when there was an explosion.

A second before the explosion, the prosecutor happened to look out of the porthole. When he saw the flash in the sky, he told himself:

Not coincidence. Chance.

The prince decrees that all citizens of (Q) must be kept in a permanent state of arousal. Punishment can only ever be given in role-play and utilising a variety of royally patented sex toys; power brokers and rebels alike will be mocked or pilloried only for their failure to arouse and be aroused.

**

Ruler and Stick

After his mother died of what they referred to as a weak heart and his father went crackers, Arturo and his sister were packed off to a school run by the priests.

In the first few months, Arturo was depressed and lonely. He began to detest the priests, and particularly the priest Vigilante who would punish all crimes and misdemeanours such as talking out of turn and making cheeky remarks with his long, bendy ruler.

The priests' school was in a small town surrounded by cherry orchards. One day, Arturo was out with a new friend looking for cherries. His friend claimed to know a really good spot where they could find the really good ones – not the easy pickings at the side of the road, but the small and sweet ones from which you could make *amarena*. His friend lost his way; they could not find the *amarena* cherries. It was hot and they sat down under some trees to get out of the sun. To Arturo's surprise his friend took down his shorts and started jerking off. His friend, who was fourteen, had a long, thin penis with very little pubic hair. Arturo who was also excited took down his shorts and started jerking off. When his friend came, Arturo stopped. Although he was perfectly capable of coming, (Arturo was thirteen and a half) he could not bring himself to do it. The following day they returned to look for the amarena cherries and jerk off. Like the day before, Arturo held back until he could no longer control himself. His friend, who was on the point of coming, asked if he could "fuck Arturo in the arse", but Arturo was too young and squeamish about the idea. His friend had to be content with his *sega*.

He of the long, bendy ruler, the priest Vigilante was something of a Jekyll and Hyde. In bible reading classes, Vigilante was holier than thou and squeaky clean for

God. When it came to doing literature, on the other hand, he would set them painful tasks such as parsing sentences, locating Greek portmanteaus, analysing subjunctive moods, and defeating them with rhetorical devices such as periphrasis and synecdoche; in short, condemning them to a hell that neither Dante nor his friend Cavalcanti could have imagined.

Vigilante's other task was to make them sweat in the "gym" – in reality, a small, musty room at the back of the cloister. They had to do handstands and headstands, while he held their legs and looked down their shorts. The catch for the younger boys was they were not allowed to wear their underpants, since this was considered "unhygienic". One day, in the middle of their exercising, Arturo pulled up short. Vigilante sent him to the changing rooms. A few minutes later, he came and put his hand down Arturo's shorts. Had he sprained his groin? – Vigilante was not only a sadist, but also a voyeur. He would come into the showers and watch. The pretext was always the same – to make sure they were washing themselves properly. God did not like dirty boys and germs. He would stand there with a distant look as if his mind was on higher things. The boys were not taken in.

They would make jokes behind his back, and yet in a funny way they accepted Vigilante's behaviour. It was the norm, like the punishment meted out with his long, bendy ruler.

When he was about fifteen and a half, and now under the guardianship of two old friends of his mother, Arturo had become "something of a tearaway" as they often put it in his reports. He was no longer interested in studying and used to hang out with the "lads" in the class.

In the class was a handicap boy whose name was Diego Rodriguez (his parents were Argentine immigrants). Diego had a speech impediment and a mental age of a ten-year old boy, or so everyone thought. Naturally, he was growing and becoming interested in the girls in the class; he asked them to show him their breasts, and sometimes he would try to flick up their skirts to see what colour knickers they were wearing. As for the girls, they were tolerant of Diego, who was considered "harmless"; in fact, they often tried to help him overcome his `mental disabilities. One of the girls, known as "Lemon" Verbena, was quite short and busty in that way of Mediterranean girls; Arturo took a fancy to her, as did the other lads. Unlike the other girls, she had a confident and indeed spiky personality. She always had a ready answer for the boys who teased her about her attributes.

Lemon Verbena wore short denim skirts and Super GA trainers that were fashionable at that time. One day, Diego Rodriguez came up behind her during break and with his ruler flicked up her skirt. As she turned round, Diego managed to get in another flick and everyone saw her panties. Lemon Verbena snatched the ruler out of Diego's hand and struck him with it across the face.

Once she had calmed down, Lemon Verbena tried to explain to Diego why she had struck him. "Don't you see, Diego, only stupid boys do things like that?"

"Quite right," said one of Arturo's friends. "We must be careful Diego doesn't get hold of that ruler again."

"Next time we should report him to Vigilante."

"Don't be stupid," said Arturo. "He needs to be educated, like you cretins."

While he was careful not to show it, Arturo had a crush on Lemon Verbena. Already with several conquests under his belt (that involved a lot of petting and fondling but no real fornicating) Arturo was still in a condition intolerable to any self-respecting leader. He would have dearly loved to remedy the situation with Lemon Verbena and lose his cherry. – If this desire now seemed unattainable after the episode with Diego, Lemon Verbena was no fool. She must have known that it was he – as the class leader – who had put Diego up to the ruler flicking trick that showed everyone her pink panties with the little frill.

However, Arturo had a plan. Guessing that the way to Lemon Verbena's heart was through the handicap boy, he began to sit with Diego in class and help him with his exercises.

Naturally, all his friends thought this was a huge joke. One day, outside school, they got it into their heads to offer Diego a cigarette. Diego had never smoked a cigarette; when he started choking on it, Arturo was furious. What did they think they were doing making him smoke? He stubbed out the cigarette and drew Diego aside. By chance, or design, Lemon Verbena happened to be walking past; his friends started taking the mickey. "Ignore those idiots," he said, turning his back on them. He walked off with Diego, who must have been pleased his new friend was going to show his collection of dirty magazines.

Over the coming weeks, Lemon Verbena began to soften in her attitude. She promised to help him with his studies.

If Arturo was a lazy student, Lemon Verbena had the best marks in class, particularly for Greek and philosophy. She had won a prize for a Socratic – to class wags Sapphic dialogue between an Amazonian princess and the ugly, old philosopher.

One afternoon Lemon Verbena was helping Arturo with his Greek homework when Lemon Verbena's boyfriend came round. Arturo went home feeling like an Achilles heel. His sister asked him what the matter was. He told her about Lemon Verbena. "Which Verbena?" She asked, since there were several Verbenas in the school. "Not the one with short hair?" she said. "No," he said, "not that sack of potatoes." After a while they managed to work out which Verbena they were talking about, and the fact that "the" Lemon Verbena's boyfriend was in his sister's class. His sister told him he had nothing to worry about. "Verbena's boyfriend is quite unbelievably religious." – "What do you mean?" –

"I mean he's best friends with the priest." – "Best friends with Vigilante. Are you sure?" – "Take it from me, Arturo. That boy is more interested in Vigilante's rosary than his girlfriend's attributes." On hearing this from his sister, Arturo got his hopes up; if Lemon Verbena was living the lie of enforced chastity, he surely stood a chance.

Lemon Verbena was not only a model student, but she was also the star of the local basketball team. Cool under pressure, she was not only good at taking penalties but also highly adept at dribbling around those tall earnest girls who wore glasses and ponytails.

Arturo embarked on a new stratagem which involved taking Diego along to watch Lemon Verbena' basketball matches. He didn't care when his friends started teasing him about becoming the head cheerleader. This was in the days when girls did not have the luxury of those upright sports bras, but ones that allowed their breasts to bounce around freely. If Diego was happy as a bunny watching all those bouncing breasts, and his hand went his trousers, Arturo turned a blind eye.

To help with her training and endurance, Arturo suggested they go running together. Diego, of course, wanted to come too. Diego was pretty unfit, so they left him, short of breath, on a bench and set off again. They ran past the cherry orchards – those very orchards, it turns out, where Arturo had brought off his friend, and down to the beach towards the old tower.

As chance would have it, it started bucketing down. They headed for the tower and huddled in the doorway to shelter from the rain. Arturo took off his T-shirt and rang it out. "Why don't you do the same?"

"Don't be silly," she said.

On the ground in the abandoned tower were a lot of sticks and rubbish. "Here," he said, "I know a trick to light a fire."

He went to pick up one of the sticks. "Give me that," she cried, snatching it out of his hand.

They tussled with the stick until it snapped. "Idiot," she said, "how are we going to build your fire now?"

Lemon Verbena picked up another stick. Arturo went to grab the second stick. The stick caught on his shorts.

Lemon Verbena stopped; she looked at him. Slowly she moved the stick up inside his shorts.

Arturo closed his eyes. In his mind's eye, he pictured the long, bendy ruler Vigilante used to mete out punishment. In a fury of lust, he grabbed the stick from Lemon Verbena's hand and began to pay her back.

She closed her eyes, as he pushed the stick between her legs. Arturo knew that he was close to achieving his objective.

The novel in 28 chapters was set in a fictional – one assumes - South American country. A series of murders take place among the high-ranking officials of the government. The protagonist, a detective named Q ordered to investigate the murders can find no solution to the crimes...

***

Twenty-eight

Quibbling it may be, but it's hard to imagine, from the outside, the lengths to which one may go to get one's reward...

A few days before her exam, Betty asked her father for some money for a new dress.

Although her father was not exactly the richest man in town, any more than he believed in throwing money around, he did not like to see his daughter looking like a tramp. Appearances were as important to him as they were to her. He reached into his pocket and took out his wallet.

"Thank you, papa," she said, and gave him a kiss.

Her father went back to reading his newspaper and she returned to her bedroom to get ready to go out.

Later, she met her boyfriend in the centre and they went to look for the dress.

After much debate, and indeed trial and error, visiting several shops where she was on familiar terms with the shop assistants, and who tried to get her to buy things that were not quite appropriate, or nearly appropriate, she settled on a grey trouser suit. Her boyfriend offered to pay; she was relieved. "Are you sure about it?" she said, as he pulled out his wallet.

"Anyway," he said, "you're always saying I'm a rich bastard."

Betty laughed.

"Do I really say that?" she said, as if surprised, though, in fact, by her standards, he was not poor. Not only did he have a regular job but he also owned his own flat. He was, as the saying goes, *sistemato*, sorted for life.

The following day, dressed in the grey trouser suit, she arrived at the faculty.

Students were still milling around outside the exam hall; she stopped to talk to a friend. Are you going to sit for it?

"I don't know," said her friend. "I haven't really studied."

"Me, too," she said. "I don't feel ready."

"You always say that," said her friend." You always get a good mark."

"Don't talk rubbish!"

"I mean it. I'm going to fail."

"Don't be ridiculous! You always wangle it in the end."

Another friend had come over to join in the discussion. In spite of the fact that they all said they had not studied and were not ready to do the exam, they went and sat at the back of the hall. While they waited for the commission to arrive, they talked shop and exam horror stories.

"Remember that time Professor Intanti was helping his wife feed the baby in the room next to the exam hall."

"What about that time the caretaker went on holiday and we had to climb over the gate to get in? – I laddered my tights!"

"That was too ridiculous!"

"We'll never pass our degrees."

"What does it matter? There won't be any jobs anyway."

Finally, the commission arrived.

The head of the commission, who was the professor of constitutional law, had the reputation for being a hard taskmaster. He never gave away questions; he liked you to be able to quote articles from memory. If you missed a phrase, or failed to use the correct subjunctive, he was merciless with sarcasm. A good mark for his exam was twenty-eight. He rarely gave thirty; very exceptionally, according to wags in the faculty, he would give thirty plus to the well-prepared sons and daughters of his colleagues.

If she knew that thirty was quite beyond her, Betty still hoped that with a bit of luck she would get twenty-eight. She wanted the twenty-eight to keep her average. At the back of this she had plans – plans to go on doing research. Although she did not believe in the value of research per se, she thought of it as a way to stave off the inevitable. Besides, she was tired of living at home.

It was her turn to do the exam; she sat down and took a deep breath. The exam, she thought, had not gone badly. She was pleased with her skill in negotiating all the traps set for her. It was not a perfect exam, but she thought she had deserved her twenty-eight.

She got up and went to the desk where the professor was beginning to write out the mark against her name. When he asked for her libretto so that he could record her mark, she made her excuses to the professor.

On the way out of the exam hall, she met her friend who wanted to know what mark she had managed to wangle, but B was in a hurry.

"I left my libretto home," she said. "I've got to go and get it."

"Oh, dear," said her friend. "I hope the professor isn't angry."

"I hope not," she said.

When Betty arrived home, her father, who was in the living room, asked her how much she got in the exam. Betty told him a white lie. There had been too many students. She would have to return the following day.

"My poor girl," he said. "After all you have studied."

"Well, papa," she said. "I'll just have to hope the professor is in a better mood tomorrow."

Betty went into her room and opened her wardrobe. After some deliberation, she took out several dresses and skirts. She stood in front of the mirror, holding each item of clothing before her. When she had settled on a short brown suede skirt, she picked out a white polo neck and a pair of white tights from the chest of drawers. When she was ready, she looked in her desk drawer for a white envelope.

It was five o'clock when the professor finished the exams; Betty was sitting on a chair outside his office.

"Good evening, Signorina," he said, as he unlocked the door. He took the folded *verbale* and spread it on his desk. He began to scrutinise the names.

Betty slipped the white envelope onto the table. The professor made no sign that he had seen it. "Signorina," he said, "I must compliment on your exam. It was very well done."

The professor handed back the libretto and she thanked him.

Afterwards, she had arranged to meet her boyfriend in the centre. "Knock me dead," he said when she came over. "What happened to the trouser suit?"

He wrapped his hands around her waist and kissed her on the lips. "By the way," he said, holding her tightly and squeezing her bum, "how much did the dirty bastard give you?"

When she told him, he grinned and said:

"You must be pleased."

Betty, however, was not pleased; she wanted to burst into tears. She did not feel she had deserved twenty-eight.

You may well ask why I look to the horizon when my little ship is adrift in the gutter.

***

The English Teacher

When Achille Lombardo told me he had started doing English lessons, I laughed my head off. If I was the worst in the class at school, Achille Lombardo was not far behind. "Achille," I said. "Remember our teacher, Signora Tarantini used to say we were tone deaf." "Speak for yourself, Cassa. You were the tone deaf one. I just could not be bothered to study for that old shrew." If, however, Achille Lombardo was perfectly serious about his English lessons; it was because of his English teacher.

Achille was a busy man, of course. He was often away in Milan and Rome. He organised his lessons for the early mornings and late evenings. Often, of course, he would cancel; it became a running joke between them – his cancellations and her chastisements for his tardiness, his inability, what's more, to knuckle down and learn his irregular verbs and the lists of lexical items she set him for homework. In the end, he took her out to the Due Ghiottone where they sat contemplating the vast quantities of antipasti and drank the Verdecca that he had ordered to go with it. There began a period of courtship in which he began to practice his English quite seriously. His English teacher lived in a flat with three other females – all, single, pharmacy students. Two were quite ugly, he told me; the other small and pretty who on other occasions he would not have minded flirting with. In the evenings when they came in from their walks along the seafront; they would offer him a strawberry liqueur, which after a while he began to decline, just as she would his advances. Then, one day he managed to extract a longer, steamier kiss on the doorstep. It was two o'clock in the morning, and he went home happy.

It was fireworks night. Every year on the ninth of May fireworks are held in honour of our town's patron saint.

- Our patron saint who everyone knows as Father Christmas but whose bones we stole from the Turks...

Achille Lombardo had organised a party as he did every year on his terrace to watch the fireworks, but everything - as usual – was running late. The boats were out on the water, and the crowds were waiting down below. They were still waiting for the fireworks when his English teacher turned up with her friends - a Scottish couple (he made the mistake of calling them English) and a girl who he thought was American but turned out to be Canadian. They were all teachers, of course. – Immediately he got this sense that something was wrong; partly because the Canadian girl who had a stud in her nose and was wearing a pair of army boots looked pretty pissed or pissed off about something. It transpired the English couple – or rather the Scottish couple had had all their money stolen. (They had kept the money in a cupboard in their room! Not even under the mattress.) In fact, they were going off in the morning, on their motorbike back to Scotland. He felt bad about this. Here we go again with our reputation for thievery and general skulduggery. He was trying to explain. The bones of the saint had been stolen from the Turks and now it was happening again to this nice English/Scottish couple who'd come here to teach their language. He sincerely wished them well, and wanting them to have a good time before they went away on their motorbikes back to Scotland, he picked up a bottle of champagne and popped the cork. As he did, the cork flew up in the air and hit the Canadian girl on the head, which was quite funny, especially when his friend De Santis started jumping up and down, trying to explain. "It means you're going to get married," he was saying. The Canadian girl didn't understand. "I don't want to get married," she said. – She looked completely baffled as well as indignant. And then he turned round and started talking to his English teacher. "I hope your friends are all right?" He said. "Don't worry," she said. "They're having a good time." But it was too late. De Santis had started talking to the Canadian girl in his terrible English. The Canadian girl didn't really seem very amused. She kept looking up at the sky and asking when were they going to let off the fireworks? De Santis had become transfixed by the Canadian girl's army boots. He wanted to try them on. The Canadian girl couldn't believe it. "Is he drunk?" she said. De Santis kept insisting. Marika his wife who could speak English was saying. "Don't worry," she said. "He's an embarrassment to me, too." The Canadian shrugged and took her boots off. De Santis took off his loafers. De Santis started walking round in her army boots. – The Canadian girl, poor thing, couldn't get into his loafers. Suddenly the sky above the old town burst into light. Achille Lombardo leaned over and whispered in Julia's ear if she would care to come round the following night and sleep in his bed. "You will promise?" he said. We watched the fireworks. It was a good show, possibly better than the previous year. The party began to break up. He said goodbye to Julia and her unhappy friends. When everyone had gone, he collapsed in a chair and fell asleep. When he woke up the next morning, he was still holding the stub of his cigar.

All through May, cloudless skies seemed to lie over the old town, above the tangle of aerials and starched linen. Old men stood on street corners, talking politics and football with the same tedious passion. Bored young men sipped beers outside bars, watching the traffic of inaccessible girls walking by in short skirts and sandals. Fliers of suited politicos littered the pavements and bunged up the gutters. If there was a buzz in the air, it was not just the buzz of the changing seasons. The buzz of an election, the placards of progress, and the platitudes of change seemed to peel away from the shutters and boarded up shop-fronts of his boring, provincial town.

In the coming days, she came round to his flat every lunch time, just as Achille Lombardo would return from the courts. There was next to nothing to eat. All he had in his fridge was a couple of bottles of Prosecco and a bottle of Campari left over from the party, some olives and crisps. So they would pop down to the delicatessen for some rolls and mortadella. They would take them back upstairs and they would sit out on the terrace. He would mix her a spritz. "You know what the secret of a good spritz is," he said. "Strawberries. Tomorrow I must get some strawberries." So, they would sit eating their rolls of *mortadella* and drinking their spritz with olives until it was time for her to go off to her lessons.

People of course were phoning up all the time, but Achille Lombardo did not care. He would let his mobile ring; when it stopped ringing, he would pick it up and look to see who had phoned. He did not want to phone them back, and mostly he didn't. – He was happy just to watch Julia as she stood by the wall looking back at him smiling her inscrutable smile and holding her spritz. For if this was a time of pledging votes building alliances, it was a game he had been playing for a long time. – And yet in all this, he could not help thinking, as Julia stood by the wall, looking back at him, smiling her inscrutable smile, that it was quite foolish. For what did he care if they had his vote or not? – He did not give one jot. Then he would call to her:

"Will you marry me?"

Realising as he popped the question, he was bubbling over just like the spritz.

It was a hot day, the first really hot day of the year, when they drove out to see the church. The priest was immediately suspicious. Charmed by his church, they explained they wanted to get married there. The conversation seemed to be going nowhere, but they wanted to see the church anyway. The priest took them to see the side chapel. The saint's relics were contained in a glass cabinet. They were he explained relics that were particularly useful in cases of infertility, and if a male heir was desired. They looked quite kitsch, she whispered. He said, in all innocence, it would make a nice present for the saint. Perhaps the priest didn't believe him, but he was amused. Not only was he amused, but he also knew the visitor was going to fix the roof of his chapel. (Actually, it did need some work and never got enough from the parish because it was a poor parish and he was that rare breed - a kind, un-manipulative priest).

On the day of the wedding, a team of florists came from town to decorate the baroque altar. The bride and groom turned up in a chauffeur driven Mercedes Benz. The priest made her translate the ceremony. When they took vows, his English teacher made a joke only the English guests got ("I promise," she said, "to be faithful for as long as I can"). The reception was held down on the coast in a very stylish hotel with a swimming pool and a live band who played a mixture of jazz and old Beatles and Rolling Stones hits (with terrible accents according to the English guests). The photographer was from the local gazette; apart from her friends like Suzy and her daughter Amber, they were mainly his friends, local VIPs (such as the De Gennaros) and old dear friends of his father and mother (such as Scoditti and Garolla). Both his parents were dead – a car accident many years ago I heard. Her mother didn't come of course; and her father – well, she didn't bother to contact him because they hadn't seen each for several years now. The bride they said was very beautiful; she spoke exquisite Italian with barely a trace of an accent. There was a lot of dancing. As usual, his friend, De Santis made everyone laugh with his imitation of John Travolta spinning around under an imaginary go-go to Night Fever.

For their honeymoon, they had planned to go to America. As this was just after 9/11, however, they could not get a visa; Achille suggested Mexico, but his English teacher said she just wanted to do something local, so they went on a driving holiday in Tuscany and Umbria. The truth was his English teacher was in love with Italy. They stayed in luxury hotels with views of the lakes and ate truffles, or truffles and pasta in luxury restaurants. They visited churches and cathedrals and saw lots of paintings by old Medieval and Renaissance masters. She wrote him a short poem, which she decided not to give him; instead, she put it in the back of notebook and forgot all about it.

When they got back from the honeymoon, they moved into the villa. The villa had been in Achille Lombardo's family for several generations. He'd had it done up – not quite to his English teacher's taste - there was a Jacuzzi in the bottom bathroom with gold taps and seashells encased in the tiles. Yet who could resist the narrow winding staircase that led to the small tower where you looked out over the vineyards, olive groves, and cherry orchards?

They had a maid, Milly. Her husband, Benny looked after the garden and security.

Besides the alarm system, there were five CCT cameras, one going down the north wall, the other trained on the west wall, one on the pool and the terrace. Since he'd been making money from his sofa business – by profession, he was actually a commercial lawyer -, he'd also begun an art collection. Among Italian contemporary artists, he had a small peasant scene from Gattuso's late period and a little-known Mons Venus by Pino Pascoli. There were also two cabinets full of

Etruscan and Roman vases, plus some pieces from Magnia Grecia, including a diadem that was thought to belong to a Dauanian princess. One felt Achille Lombardo was proud of all these objets d'art.

By his own account Achille had wanted her to stop working, but his English teacher told him she did not want to give up her life. Being who he was, he managed to wangle her a job as a *lettore* or reader in an Italian school where she was it seemed pretty content, even if at times it was – as she put it - more taxing teaching teenage girls with boy problems and period pains than businessmen with portfolios and planes to catch. Frankly, I wondered, what was she doing there? – She was not made for English classes, any more than Achille was made for a sofa business.

For Christmas, I understand, they went to England. There had been no time to see her friends; instead, they went to stay with the dreaded mother-in-law. I forgot to mention the dreaded mother-in-law. Although invited to the wedding, she had refused to come. Achille had been murky on the reasons; personally, I believe she was an old soak. In spite of everything, at Christmas, the mother-in-law had been on her best behaviour. And Robin was charm itself; he and Achille got on well with their gin and tonics, and their rambling thoughts about rugby football and the state of international affairs. They went to a New Year's party at the boatyard. His mother-in-law became quite distraught; she regretted not coming to the wedding. Mother and daughter kissed and made up; and that seemed to be the end of it he thought, even if they didn't speak very much on the phone.

All this happened just over a year ago; they were settling down, it seemed, into a life of domestic bliss: when Achille phoned me up and said:

"She's left me."

"You fool," I said. In the next breath: "Why should she have done that?"

"I have no idea," he said. "There was no letter in the envelope, only her set of keys."

"Well," I said, "at least you won't have to change the locks."

Outsider

Of course, they did not know they were going to become lovers. It seemed to come off quite naturally, without inhibition, one day when they were on their way to the beach...

They drove along the coast road, past villas and restaurants on the outskirts of the town. At length they came to a barrier. They parked the car, got their beach bags from the boot and climbed over the barrier. Here, the road was cracked in places and in danger of falling into the sea. Back from the road, on the slight incline of a hill, was an abandoned property comprising a turreted villa and several outhouses. At the bottom of the slope, by a broken fence, was the tired-looking skull of a swimming pool.

The villa, he said, was the property of a famous recluse... a rich lady, who also kept dogs and let local children swim in the pool. The lady would never appear.

"Did you swim in her pool?"

"Only once. I got frightened off by the dogs."

"Poor boy."

As it was full of plastic bags and beer bottles, they did not care to stop in the first cove. Instead, they carried on walking along the cliff path where they met a teenage boy who nearly fell off his scooter when he hit a rock and started cursing in that way teenage boys do. As if it was the fault of the rock and not the boy's impatient revving of his scooter. "Be quiet," he said, "he'll hear you!" – "Well," she said, stifling her giggles, "it serves him right for being such a show off!"

At length they came to a wall with barbed wire running along the top, and they could walk no further along the cliff. The woman was curious to know what was behind it. She clambered over the rocks trying to see around the side of the wall. Then she said as a dare they should try and climb over the wall. But the man said it was not a good idea.

"Why on earth not?"

"Well, for a start that barbed wire is very old and rusty."

She laughed and called her lover chicken. "Why chicken?" – Chicken, she explained, was what English children said to each other when they didn't want to dare. "To us," he said, "it was forbidden. We were not allowed to go beyond the wall."

"So," she said, "all you children were chickens."

Against her protests, he led her by the hand back along the cliff to the cove they had just passed.

There was an old iron ladder down onto the beach. The final steps were so rotten they had to jump with their beach bags onto the sand.

The seaweed had come up onto the beach, and they had to make a little path with their feet so they could sit without being disturbed by sand flies.

Happily, she wriggled out of her jeans and walked down to the edge of the shore. The water was cold when she put in her toes.

She stood in the water enjoying the sensation. Then she put her hands in, scooped some water and washed her face.

She walked back to where he was sitting smoking a cigarette. She took off her top and lay back.

The man leaned over and kissed her breasts. Then he got up and took off his shorts. He went down to the shore and waded out up to the bottom of his black trunks; then he came back to the beach to take off his T-shirt. Venturing out again, he took the plunge and dived under water. She watched as his head rose and then dipped again.

He swam out to a rock at the edge of the cove. The rock was about a hundred metres away. She watched him moving away from her in the water. He disappeared around the rock. For a while she could not see him.... She began, foolishly, to worry until she saw his head rising again in the water on the far side of the rock. When he reached the beach, he was out of breath. Then he came and sat down on the sand, next to her.

"Anyway," he said, "if we never did climb the wall, I knew someone who did. He was not from around here."

"What was his name?"

"We didn't know his name. To us he was just an outsider."

"Because he was different?"

He made no attempt to answer her question; instead he began to tell her this apocryphal story.

'In those days the Queen's House was surrounded by a perimeter. The perimeter was at times characterised by a wall, at times by a fence with barbed wire with guards positioned along its length. No outsider could enter the perimeter. If captured, they were taken prisoner and locked away in the palace.

One day, the protagonist of my story was guarding the top of the perimeter where you could see the woods and the hills about. If it was lonely at the top of the perimeter, the young guard held her spear tighter and thought of her duty to protect the Queen.

The young guard returned from her watch to find the guardroom in an uproar. "What is all the fuss about?" She asked.

"Didn't you hear?" Some said. "We have taken a prisoner."

Most of the guards were too young to know an outsider. They asked one of the older guards what they were like.

The old guard shrugged. "They are different from us," she said. "They behave differently, both in their movements and their manners, although of course we are the same species."

The young guards were confused by the old guard's explanation. "You are talking in riddles," they said. "Why don't you say something more intelligent?"

The old guard took time to consider her answer. "They are like strangers. They may talk like us, but they lie and insinuate. You can't trust them."

The younger guards were puzzled. "What did the outsiders do to make them so untrustworthy?"

The old guard smiled.

They realised the old guard was teasing them… "In truth," she said, "I have never met an outsider, although I heard a rumour once. – An outsider came to talk to our Queen. He made her an offer she could not refuse."

"Well," said one of the young guards, "I cannot imagine that."

"In fact," said the old guard, "the Queen was a wily campaigner, but the outsider was very persistent.

"What did he want?" She asked.

"He said that he would give her many fine wares if she would marry him. The Queen replied she did not need fine wares. The outsider said he would give her many diamonds. This scene of diplomacy continued for a while. The court could see the outsider was getting frustrated; he threw up his hands in a gesture of despair. Finally, he said he had something important to tell our Queen but he would not reveal it unless her guard was removed from the hall."

The young guards were shocked. "What! No guards around the Queen! Who did he think he was?"

They conferred amongst themselves about this unusual precedent. The old guard remained silent.

The young guards wanted to know what happened.

"It is said the outsider spent the night with the Queen. In the morning he disappeared."

Over the following days, the young guard heard little more of the outsider. She was on a guard duty in the palace – first in the queen's vault and then in her bedchambers. When she came back to the guardroom, she had little time for rumour and gossip. She fell fast asleep.

When, in the morning, she went to look at the duty roster, she saw it was her turn to guard the prisoner. She went to the outsider's cell. She looked in the cell, but the outsider was lying on his bed with his face to the wall. Over him was a blanket. She could not satisfy her curiosity. She took up her position before the cell and waited. As she stood there, she could hear him moving around behind her. She did not dare turn round. Her heart began to beat faster; she felt she was going to faint. Every time she did she tried to pull herself together and remember her duty. It was then that she felt his breath on the back of her neck – his voice in her ear. She jumped and turned round – putting up her sword and shield. "Avast!" She cried. "Stand back!"

The outsider was looking at her; there was laughter in his eyes.'

"What has happened?" – "There was a gas explosion next door in the *salumeria*. Now, Doctor Noviello is selling his flat." – "*Rompiscatole*, what am I going to do with this box?"

***

Kind Doctors

"What has happened?" – "There was a gas explosion next door in the *salumeria*. Now, Doctor Noviello is selling his flat." – "*Rompiscatole*, what am I going to do with this box?"

One day, about a year prior to this conversation in front of some scaffolding in via Carulli, two boys were on their way to Doctor Noviello's flat. Between them, they were dragging a suitcase across the busy road up by the San Giuseppe Church when a Vespa pulled up onto the pavement. The boys, out of alarm, dropped their case. With them was an older man, who called out:

"Boys, watch your backs."

This was the famous Doctor Amir formerly of Gaza City, who now worked as a dental assistant.

Doctor Amir came round behind one of the boys and picked up a boot that had fallen out of his rucksack... "They'll steal these boots if you're not careful," he said. "They'll steal their own mother's boots."

As they went on their way, Doctor Amir was still counselling the two boys:

"Another thing you must remember, boys. Italians are not always on time. In fact, I would say they are not the best of timekeepers, which of course does not mean to say you should not be on time. You must be on time, even if they are not on time."

As if to prove the point, when Doctor Amir rang the bell, Doctor Noviello was not at home.

Dr Amir rang the bell a second time. He took his phone out of his pocket and dialled Doctor Noviello's number... Ah, they were in luck. A friend of Doctor Noviello, another doctor who lives in the same building as Doctor Noviello, could let them in.

Doctor Moro, who lived in the flat below Doctor Noviello, could not have been more kind. He invited them into his flat and offered them a coffee. While they waited for Doctor Noviello, he engaged them in conversation. Usually it was Marco, as opposed to Hamid, who answered; Doctor Moro could not have been more impressed. "Marco," he said, turning and winking at Doctor Amir, "speaks our language better than my giddy aunt."

"You are very kind, Doctor Moro," said Marco, who was easily flattered. "My Italian is very poor. It will improve with your help."

"Mo', guaion', che si dic'?" (Mate, what's up?)

"Rompiscatole, che fai?" (Box breaker, what you doin'?)

Doctor Noviello, who was a rather small man, was holding a rather large box. They shook hands all round.

"O', ragazzi, ma chin'." (Boys, let's go!)

Still holding onto his box, Doctor Noviello took them up to his flat and into a room full of yet more boxes.

"Aspe'! Dobbiamo spostare tutti questi rompiscatole!" (Lit. Wait! We got to move all these ball breaking boxes!)

Before they could move in, the boys had to move the boxes out of the room into another room which also turned out to be full of boxes. And yet, Doctor Noviello could not have been more kind.

"*Ragazzi, siete molto gentili*! – *Non dimenticare di chuidere il gas!*" (Boys, you are very kind! – Don't forget to turn off the gas!)

The following day Dr Noviello took the boys along to the Questura to organise their permessi. Dr Noviello, who was on intimate terms with the clerk, fixed everything up and showed them how to fill in the "quiz". The clerk gave them a chit (*pezzo di carta*) they were to produce when they came back for their permessi.

On the way home they stopped off at the market and bought some *cozze* (mussels) and *datteri* (dates). Doctor Noviello prepared lunch (PRAN-zo) in honour of his new guests (*ospiti*). He invited Doctor Moro and his girlfriend, his amic-A, Marika and of course Dr Amir. Doctor Noviello cooked spaghetti (al dente) with mussels and dates. The dates were a special treat "a-bus-I-vo" for his guests. Marika had made a cream cake (pan di Spagna), and Doctor Moro brought some wine (pri-mi-TI-vo).

In the evening Doctor Amir took the boys off to the mosque in the cellar on the other side of the city. Dr Amir knew of a shop where they sold flour (*farina*) and sesame seed paste (*crema di semi di sesame*). The boys made some unleavened bread (*pane sensa lievito*) and hummus; even Hamid began to feel better about life.

The boys soon settled down and went to lectures at the medicine faculty. Sometimes they went to lunch at Doctor Amir's flat and tasted his wife's rice (RI-zo). They settled into a routine, studying together and going to the mosque in the cellar. They made their unleavened bread and hummus. On one occasion, they were invited down to Doctor Moro's flat. Doctor Moro cooked them risotto with seafood: clams (von-GO -le) and baby prawns (*gamberetti*). Although they ate it, neither Hamid nor Marco really liked the way he had done the *rizo*. Doctor Noviello was often busy – either moving boxes or making long distance phone calls to a lady (Signora Rompiscatole) in New York (regarding the contents of his boxes). He found time to take care of Doctor Amir's parking fine (*multa*) and sort the chit of their *permessi* with his friend the clerk.

In the context of such kindness (*gentilezza!*) the months passed. One day the boys were studying in their room in the flat; Marco began to sing a song. It was an old song sung by his mother. (Marco was not nostalgic in a sad way but merely happy at the thought of his childhood among the olive groves by the sea). Hamid could contain himself no more. "Why are you singing that song?"

"Don't you like my singing?"

"No, as a matter of fact, I don't like your singing. It's getting on my nerves… *Mi fai incazzare.*"

"Doctor Noviello likes my singing…"

Marco began to wax about the evening when they had all been singing those Neapolitan love songs: Napule', I so pazz', Te voglio bene assaje, L'ammore ca'nun vene… Marco had sung a lullaby (*ninna nanna*) and he had tried to teach Doctor Noviello the words.

"Why do you call him a doctor? His name is Noviello. Signor Noviello."

"Everyone in this country is a doctor. Soon we will become doctors."

An argument broke out between the two friends. "Anyway, why do you call yourself Marco? Your name is not Marco. Your name is Marik."

Marco wrinkled his brow. "Italians don't understand Arab names," he said. "I give myself a new name. What of it!"

Tempers frayed. Hamid accused Marco of making eyes at Doctor Moro's girlfriend. Marco accused Hamid of accusing him of such dishonourable behaviour. Hamid cursed Italy and declared he was leaving. "I do not want to stay here anymore," he said. "Italy is a heathen place."

"Italy is not a heathen place," said Marco. "It is heavenly."

To annoy Hamid, he broke into heavenly song. Hamid got up to leave. "Where are you going?"

"Well," said Hamid. "It's time to go to the cellar."

Marco refused to accompany him; instead, he sat in the room studying to be a doctor. What's more, a kind, Italian doctor. - Not a cruel, Arab doctor like Hamid.

Shortly after this, Doctor Amir came over to see what all the fuss was about.

"Why does he want to leave? - I told him Italy is a beautiful country. His future is here. He won't listen to me, Doctor Amir."

Although he could see it was going to be an uphill struggle trying to keep the peace, Doctor Amir gave what he thought was a rather fine speech all about kindness, gentility and the Hippocratic Oath. None of these arguments, however, seemed to hold much water with Hamid; his mind was made up. He was going to get the slow boat home.

Neither Dr Amir nor Dr Noviello could make it to the ferry; Dr Moro very kindly offered to drive the boys down to the port.

As he picked his bag off the back seat, Hamid, one could tell, was dragging his feet. He turned to Doctor Moro, who slapped him on the back. "*Bravo, ragazzo!*" (Nice one, mate!)

Thanking Doctor Moro for his kindness, Hamid began to extemporize on the feelings of his heart. One day, God willing, he would return to Italy. "Italy," he said, "was a country like no other."

In the middle of this speech, Marco winked at Doctor Moro who turned away to light his cigarette; the estranged friends embraced.

"I told you," Marco said on the way home, "he is going to come back to become a doctor."

One evening, not long after this, in need of assistance regarding the boxes double-parked in his car below, Doctor Noviello knocked on Marco's bedroom door. The room was in darkness and he turned on the light. – "Marco, *che c'e?*" (What's going on?) "*Rompiscatole!*"

Marco was lying on his bed, with his face to the wall.

No amount of kindness on Doctor Noviello's part could change the fact a bomb had exploded in his hometown.

There is a fine line between the high wire and a disappearing act. - Mr. Kite

***

The Jumper

When she arrived at the airport, her husband was standing on the curb with his suitcase and mobile phone. She waved and called him. He looked up and saw her. Smiling through his conversation – he started walking towards the car.

She opened up the boot and he put the case in.

He was going to get in beside her; then changed his mind. He came round her side and as she moved over, he got in the driver's seat. He drove fast up to the hump and braked. As they went up and over the second hump, she asked how he was; he told her he was tired but exhilarated.

The trip had gone well. It seemed the company in the north was happy to liaise in what he described – using the English expression – as a joint venture.

It was late when they got home. The maid whose night off it was had left something in the fridge, but her husband wasn't hungry. They took his suitcase upstairs to the bedroom.

He opened the case and undid the dividers.

The present was in a plain black box. Inside was a green dress: very simple, but exquisitely cut. "You shouldn't have," she said. "You must have spent a fortune."

"I hope it fits," he said.

She took off her jeans, and sweatshirt, and pulled the dress over her head. She stood back to look at herself in the mirror. He came up behind her and touched her lightly on the neck. She leaned back; he bent down to kiss her.

"It's perfect," she said. "What about the shoes?"

"I already thought about those," he said, describing a pair of heels in her wardrobe.

The following night, at a small dinner party with some of his male friends, she had worn the dress to please her husband. At first, she felt uncomfortable as though the men were looking at her and undressing her with their minds.

It was one of those parties where people got quickly drunk. To hide the fact that she was flustered, she sought to distract them with neutral conversation, but they ignored her efforts. They all seemed locked in a battle of wits to impress her. The repartee was particularly sharp. She detected something in her husband's tone that she did not like. Because she did not like scenes, she got up to go into the kitchen.

When she came back with a dish, however, everyone was laughing. It was relaxed, uninhabited laughter.

Among the guests was an actor who her husband had known from school but with whom he had lost touch. The actor was touring the provinces with a production of Uncle Vanya.

"My character is like being stuck in a room with a maiden aunt polishing a gun, while everyone frets around me," he said.

Everyone laughed.

The actor was excellent company; like most actors, he had a number of funny anecdotes involving actors, celebrities and people who were famous for simply being famous.

The dinner party appeared to be a success; the guests went away, she thought, in a happy state of inebriation, and with the sour note of the early evening forgotten.

They went upstairs to bed. Her husband stood by the dresser, while she took off her earrings.

"I thought it went well," he said.

"Apart from the sticky patch at the beginning."

"You did a good job," he said. "That lot can be tricky sometimes."

She mentioned the actor who seemed to be the life and soul of the party. "Actually," said her husband, "he's miserable, having recently split with his wife in an acrimonious divorce."

"Who's his lawyer?"

"Avocado Cassa."

"Why do you call him that?"

"Oh, it's an old joke. We used to say he had adenoids."

"Well," she said, "he does a very good job of hiding it."

"Who? Avocado Cassa?"

"Your actor… he's very entertaining. I wish I had half his talent."

"My wife has other talents."

Her husband's voice trailed off, as he looked at her. The colour was in his cheeks, but she knew what he wanted. Wanting to please him, she let the dress slip to the floor and stepped out of it, and walked over to the bed in her heels.

Without saying anything, she lay down on the bed with her back to him. She felt his hands wrapping round her body. As she raised her bottom in the air, he pulled down her panties. Shortly, she felt his penis between her legs, then his shortening breath.

She was still in a state of arousal when he came. She fell asleep only to be woken from a nightmare involving her husband. They were in a flat she did not recognise. She had a feeling it was very high up, not exactly in a skyscraper, nevertheless a tall block of flats. They were with someone that they both knew but could not see. At some point, the friend said, "I'm going to jump". She woke up just as his mind seemed to be set, and she saw him leaping from the window.

By now she was wide-awake, and knew she would not go back to sleep. She went down into the kitchen to get a glass of water. Then she went into the room they used as a study. But since she was not in the mood to read, and her mind was now clear, she took out the notebook where she used to write her journal, or as she was coming to think of it as her Q book.

Her husband did not have to go away for the rest of week; he spent most of the day in the office, and when he came home in the evening, his mind was still on his work. She tried to distract him, but it was no good. Someone kept phoning up and he kept disappearing into the study to check something on the internet. Eventually she got bored, went upstairs, and made a long-distance phone call.

When he came upstairs, she was still on the phone; she became aware of him waiting for her to finish her conversation. If she was irritated, she did not show it.

She felt his hand around her neck, as she pulled up her hair. He did not have any success with the clasp, so she did it herself, putting the necklace down on the dresser.

"Who was that on the phone?"

"A friend."

"A friend?"

"You met once."

She began to contextualise their meeting; suddenly interested, he leaned over and whispered in her ear.

"Don't be silly," she said. "We didn't do things like that."

"Don't believe you. Anyway," he said, lying back on the pillow, "I seem to have forgotten. – You never told me what she looked like."

"Use your imagination."

"I haven't got an imagination. – You told me yourself. I may not have a good imagination but I've got a good memory."

Again he leaned over and whispered something in her ear, which she pretended not to hear.

"*Porco*," she said, poking him in the stomach, "you're putting on weight."

He looked at her with feigned indignation, but she kept up the line of attack.

"You must go on a diet," she said. "Eat less protein, less lust."

"I don't like the sound of that."

"Less protein," she said, putting her hand on his thigh. "It's good for you."

Someone phoned on his mobile; he got up and went to answer it. She watched him talking into the mobile.

He disappeared into the other room. A few minutes later, he came back into the room with some documents.

He spoke sharply into the phone. His voice went loud. He spoke quickly - then hung up.

"I was right," she said. "Soon you won't be able to see your balls."

"Wife," he said, wearing a wounded expression. "That's not true."

"What you need is a sound regimen," she said.

"What's that?" He said. "It sounds frightening."

Now she was lying across him with her elbow resting on his stomach scrutinising his face. "You didn't shave, either."

"Well," he said optimistically, "are you going to shave me now?"

"I rather think that's your job."

"My job?"

"Yes, your job."

She began to undo the buttons of his trousers.

"Is this part of the regimen?"

He pulled her down to whisper something in her ear. In her mind's eye she saw the jumper. Was she ready to leap?

Oh! Halcyon Days – Now wars are ending!
       You shall find where'er you sail
Tritons all the while attending
With a kind and gentle gale

***

The Prince of Q

On the urging of Mr. Handouchi, a merchant banker, Avocado Cassa had flown, at his own expense, to a reception given by the Prince of Q. When he arrived at the reception, all primed to discuss the Niger project, the prince of Q was not in the room. Through the course of the evening, he did not meet the prince, let alone catch sight of him. Instead, he was introduced to a number of his guests, including an American, who was in planes, various people in real estate, a civil engineer and a French academic doing a study on the Bedouins. Mr. Handouchi also wanted to introduce him to a Swiss lady living in Milan whose name was Celine, but she had disappeared over the other side of the room. "I really wanted you to meet her," he said.

They were making their way around the back of the American in planes when a small brown man in a brown suit buttonholed Mr. Handouchi. It was Mr. Handal from Beirut. Mr. Handal from Beirut had something urgent to communicate to Mr. Handouchi. "I am sorry," he said. "If I speak in my own language, I was forgetting my manners."

"Mr. Handal is developing a headset," said Mr. Handouchi.

"You mean, a handset, Mr. Handouchi," said Mr. Handal

"Forgive me," said Mr. Handouchi. "I'm not technical at the best times. At any rate, why don't you explain your handset to Avocado Cassa?"

Smiling, Mr. Handouchi made his excuses. The Prince of Q beckoned.

The gist of it was that, with the aid of a chip, calls everywhere in the Middle East would soon cost a tenth of what they did now. Avocado Cassa was just beginning to persuade himself that he could become Mr. Handal's

European representative when the major domo called them to dinner.

Avocado Cassa said goodbye to the brown man in the brown suit.

On the table was a fabulous array of delicacies. There was couscous salad in little edible baskets, scallops and king prawns, and bowls of exotic fruits, passion fruit and papayas.

Avocado Cassa's eye wandered over the gold finger curled Q in the middle of the bone china. Though not a novice of such occasions, his nose twitched at the sight of the well-known but aging pop star whose six-figure fee - to be paid by the Prince of Q to a charity of his choice seemed to ring out of the well-modulated claps.

After a brief flirtation with late seventies and eighties pop, Avocado Cassa liked to boast he knew next to nothing about music. Although he recognised some of the songs, they did not mean that much to him. The man on his left, a Mr. Hannay, another of Mr. Handouchi's clients and therefore he assumed the Prince of Q's seemed to be familiar with all of them. From time to time he would tap his foot or mouth the words. "I've seen him several times including Madison Square Gardens," he said, "but nowhere quite like this."

Avocado Cassa could not deny it. Watching the ageing diminutive pop star soft-peddle the Steinway was a strangely unsettling experience. There was almost no conversation in the room. He was used to conversation – loud conversation. It was in loud, almost deafening conversation he thrived.

Perhaps it was for this reason he made hard work of his conversation with Mr. Hannay until he realised he had no wish to talk about the Niger project. Instead, they found common ground over the baby mozzarellas soaking in their own milk. Mr. Hannay also liked an Italian cheese the name of which he couldn't remember. After several misunderstandings Avocado Cassa realised Mr. Hannay was talking about the soft cream cheese, *burrata*…

The conversation moved lightly now through cheeses: French v Italian cheeses. Avocado Cassa had to concede French cheeses were generally superior to Italian ones. They discussed wines. Although Mr. Hannay was not a connoisseur of wine, he tried in vain to convince him about southern Italian wines. "I know of a small vineyard," he said. "It would give me great pleasure to send you a case."

"You are very kind," said Mr. Hannay. In spite of his loving depiction of the hillside vines near his hometown, Avocado Cassa knew he had not convinced Mr. Hannay.

Amid polite but deafening applause, the ageing and diminutive pop star finished his set. Soon after, the party broke up; each guest was given a present by the Prince of Q of a cut glass bowl, exquisitely made by Murano.

Avocado Cassa said goodnight to Mr. Handouchi and Mr. Hannay. He went back up to his room with his present and got undressed.

The girl who knocked at his door was quite short; she had a young, brown face with big, brown eyes. The girl looked away when he looked at her. If she was embarrassed, so was Avocado Cassa.

He invited her in; the girl hesitated before stepping over the threshold.

Where was she from? he asked.

"India."

Where was her family?

"At home."

"Where was home?"

"India."

He asked her how old she was.

The girl told him she was eighteen.

Although he did not believe her, Avocado Cassa lay on the bed with a towel around his middle. As she worked the oils into his back, he began to feel incredibly relaxed. The songs from the evening's entertainment wafted back to him through the muslin drapes around the bed in a strange, but not unpleasant way.

Before the girl left, he got up to find his wallet and give her a tip. The girl shook her head.

Insisting, he handed her the note.

"By the way," he asked, "did she know the prince of Q?"

"No," she said, "she didn't. She had never met him."

The following morning, Avocado Cassa met Mr. Hannay for a working breakfast to discuss the Niger Project. While they were waiting for Mr. Handouchi, he could not help but ask about the young masseuse. Mr. Hannay was amused. The girls were supposed to be virgins, he said. Every night they became virgins again.

"The Prince of Q is a lucky man," he added. "But I wouldn't have his life for all the tea in China."

"I thought it was India."

Mr. Hannay chuckled at his joke.

"Talking of this Niger Project of yours," he said, "now all it needs is the rubber stamp from The Prince of Q."

On the way to the airport he phoned his wife and told her about the party. He told her about Mr. Handal and his handsets, and Mr. Handouchi's client, Mr. Hannay.

"I think you would like him," he said. "He's one of those ironic Englishman..."

His wife asked him if he had met the prince of Q. He told her about the present, the cut glass bowl, exquisitely made by Murano.

"Well, you must be careful with it," she said. "It would be unfortunate if it got broken on the way home."

When he got to the airport, Avocado Cassa put a lot of thought into the cut glass bowl. Should it go in his hand luggage, or should he have it put in the hold, or even sent by post? - On second, indeed third thoughts he decided to take it in his hand luggage.

In Rome, as regular fliers will know, it can be something of bother to get a connecting flight. As he passed through customs, Avocado Cassa was in a hurry and failed to notice the customs officers, since, confusingly, he was wearing a tweed jacket and not the uniform of the *dogana*.

The customs officer hauled him over, opened up his bag and took out the box with the cut glass bowl. Avocado Cassa's heart leapt.

"Please handle with care," he said. "That is a present from the prince of Q."

The new prisoner Seiko decided he did not want the top bunk, which was above the Mute's. He turned to the Mute and informed him that they were changing places. Then, he picked up the Mute's blanket and gave it to him. The Mute, however, put the blanket back on his own bunk. "Are you deaf?" said Seiko. "I told you this bunk's mine now." He pushed the Mute. The Mute fell back against the bunk. "Pick up your blanket," he said. When the fight broke out, the other prisoners thought Seiko was the one with the psychotic edge. But the Mute took them all by surprise when he caught Seiko in a half nelson. "Next time," he said, breaking his silence, "I'll break your arm."

***

Accidental Death of a Terrorist

I was lying on my bunk, which faced the back wall.

On the back wall surrounding the crucifix were some pin-ups and celebrities. There was also a cracked shaving mirror and an old shelf coming loose from the wall. On the shelf was a black tin box, a few paperbacks, some magazines, a bible and prayer book; a salt and pepper cellar and some spicy African sauce.

The table was tucked in between the bunks; there were no chairs, so we ate, except those days they allowed us into the canteen, from plastic trays resting on our laps.

In the cell with me were two Africans who I assumed were Nigerian, but they just as easily could have been Senegalese. I never found out what they'd done; at a guess, pimping without a permesso. - We got on with hand gestures and smiles. I should also mention the Mute, who as far as I could tell would not hurt a fly but they said had stabbed someone in the back.

When the pain started, I remember looking over at the Mute, who, as was his wont, looked straight through me. From the Mute I looked around at the Nigerians chatting on their bunks. I tried to get up; as I did, the blood drained away from me and I fell against the table. The last thing I saw were the pair of long and snaky patent leather shoes belonging to one of the Nigerians.

At some point they must have given me a pill; I thought it was poison. – I was delirious. I slept in fits and starts; in my dreams I dreamt of Betty lying on top of me. She had a curious expression on her face I believed at first to be benign until I realised she wouldn't let me move.

For what seemed like an age I was involved in a silent conversation with her, pleading for my release. Just as I began to suspect she would produce a knife from somewhere, though from exactly where was unclear since I believe she was naked; I woke up on my bunk facing the back wall. I could still feel the pain from where the knife had been plunged in.

That morning began, I recall, in a pleasant slumber between waking and dreaming of my mother's cakes sprinkled with hundreds and thousands and the hundreds and thousands of the girls I could never – alas - have.

When I opened my eyes, it took me a moment to register I had overslept. If I was late for work, I did not hurry. Taking care not to disturb Betty, I slipped out from under the covers, picked up a pair of trousers from the chair by the bed, went into the bathroom and threw some water over my face and under my arms. I picked up a clean shirt from the ironing board in the spare room. As there wasn't any time for a coffee, I gulped down some water from the tap. Before leaving the flat, I called to Betty in the bedroom, but I don't think she heard me. So I stuffed my tie in my jacket pocket and closed the front door.

I remember I drove fast along the boulevard – skipping from one lane to the other, sometimes tooting my horn and swerving to avoid the potholes. When I came over the bridge that takes you down towards the seafront, I took the tie from my jacket pocket. The wheel was resting between my knees and some fool was tooting behind me as I slipped through the light and missed the knot. I was still fumbling with it as I turned into the municipal car park and rolled the car into one of the spaces especially reserved for those who work in the tax office.

It was just after eight; I saw it on the wall clock as I came out of the lift. That clock was always five minutes fast, but it did not make any difference. Hardly had I sat down and pressed the buzzer on my desk; someone was standing at the booth with one of those green forms about which I was supposed to be the great – if not only "autorità". That, as they say, comes from Latin, but tax is as old as the Ancient Greeks.

It was around ten thirty when, as I did every morning, I closed my booth and went down to the fourth floor to pick up Giorgio. We took the back way out of the office and walked up the street past the barracks to the bar where we always went for our coffee break. Giorgio went to buy his pool slip; I remember I stood in the doorway smoking my cigarette and looking at the sea. There were a few clouds on the horizon, but the sea was flat. - Just right for a swim. Even though the summer was over, I wished I were down on the beach. If the water were cold, it wouldn't matter because when the sun was out in the middle of the day you would dry off anyway.

When I finished my cigarette, I walked back over to the bar to retrieve my coffee; Giorgio nudged me. In the mirror, above the bottles of Amaro and Campari, I saw a woman standing at the other end of the bar. The woman, who I could see only in profile, was talking and smiling into her mobile; there was another mobile resting on the bar top.

Then it was Giorgio told me his theory. "She must be a musician," he said.

"How do you know that?" I asked.

"The mobiles," he said.

Right on cue, we heard a ring tone that sounded not unlike Beethoven's fifth. Only it wasn't coming from the mobile on the bar top, but another one that was in her bag.

"What did I tell you?" Giorgio said. "That'll be the conductor."

I was still thinking about the woman and her conductor and all the possible permutations we had come up with, including our naughty selves, when I received the call from the clinic. A man in a puff jacket with a fur-lined collar was standing at the booth waving a green form at the glass. I remember his disgruntled expression – after several hours of waiting in my office, he had finally arrived at the front of the queue; I placed the closed sign on the desk and stood up without even bothering to apologise.

Paradoxically, as I drove along the seafront, I was not in any hurry. People will no doubt – along with all the other things – hold that against me.

I remember I parked the car down by the port. As I wandered past the fishermen and their catches – their little baskets arranged with tenderised octopus and open sea urchin, I remember I stopped to stare at the boats in the blackened water. There was a plastic bag floating, like some deflated jellyfish among the detritus. In contemplating my feelings, it wasn't even sadness or relief or exultation… If truth be known, I felt none of these things as I wandered into the trattoria and sat down at a table. Knife and fork and plate were brought to me, along with a plate of olives and a carafe of wine. I could not define my feelings unless it was to see myself floating like that plastic bag among the detritus. Then I broke a piece of bread and washed it down with some wine.

At some point, which only later would I appreciate as irony; I must have looked up and seen the lawyer De Santis. The lawyer De Santis, who has a high-pitched voice, but an infectious wit, was making one of his wry observations about the Mayor. The Mayor awards contracts to his friends; nevertheless, he is a good fellow and a member of the lodge...

As he brought his irony to bear on the Mayor, he bent down and rolled up his trouser leg. De Santis is nothing if not an accomplished comedian. He walked up and down between the tables with his trouser leg rolled up. He picked up a napkin and pretending it was an apron – just like a member of the lodge – at this point – he was standing by my table – as he brought his leg up in a kind of ridiculous dance, and banged his knee. The lawyer de Santis banged his knee. Everyone was in stitches, including the lawyer de Santis, who, whilst rubbing his knee, turned to me and asked what I thought of the sardines.

"The sardines are excellent," I told him.

The lawyer De Santis hobbled back to his table; I ordered fruit and coffee. When I finished my meal, I got up to pay. The lawyer de Santis called to me. "You are right, Arturo," he said. "The sardines are excellent."

I walked out the restaurant and crossed the square to pick up my car from under the nose of two idling policemen.

The clinic was on the other side of the railway track; I had to wait at the level crossing until the local commuter train passed. It was I remember quite empty, which is one of the pointless things about this town. Recently I heard from one of the guards the crossing has been removed. If now the traffic flows freely, the real problem is parking.

I arrived at the clinic to be greeted by a little fellow in low-slung jeans and trainers who might be considered one of those free spirits who make it their business to exploit this reality. He waved me into a space that had no lines but was deemed fit for my car. As I was not complaining, I handed over my "fee". The fellow nodded and walked off. I did not see him again.

Around the side of the clinic I found the chapel of rest, and a group of tearful looking people, none of whom I recognised. A man had his arms wrapped round a woman who was sobbing; another woman was looking on as though she was about to burst out of her jumper with the embroidered teddy. In this pitiful, muted atmosphere, I went and sat down on a low-lying wall to finish my cigarette.

The old man had been laid out in his three-piece suit, his hands resting on his paunch, or what was left of it.

It was not, however, the lack of paunch, but the face that struck me. The last time I had seen the old man he had a moustache; now there was no moustache. I remember looking at the face bereft of its moustache; all pinched around the lips and shrivelled around the cheeks. It did not look like him, but like someone I did not know, a total stranger.

I sat down to wait on one of the folding chairs that had been set out by the glass-fronted coffin and sat there with only the light from the candles, and a poster of a pastel Jesus to keep me company.

It was cold in the room; it did not seem that I had anything to say to the old man. As I did not want to be there, since no one had come, and I did not expect anyone to come, I got up and went back to the car. Then I put on the heating, turned on the radio, and listened for a while to some music that only made me feel more restless. For want of anything better to do, I got out of the car and went in search of a tobacconist.

I was away about half an hour. When I got back, I went to take another peek at the body. To my surprise, there were three women, dressed in fur-coats, sitting on the folding chairs beside the body.

As there was no chair for me, I stood in the doorway nursing a cigarette. None of the old women seemed to pay me much attention. I tried to make eye contact, but either they refused it or looked through me.

When I was a child, the old man taught me to play sweep with a Neapolitan deck. The money cards are the trump cards, and the sevens always lucky. You play several hands, and when you have enough trump card points or sevens, someone declares you the winner. The old man liked this game, but more than anything else, he liked winning. He always made sure he beat me until one day I got on a lucky streak and had my revenge. The old man did not like it one bit when he saw me jumping up and down. "Okay, you won once," he said. "Let's see if you can do it again." He invited me for a re-match. This time he beat me hands down; and I threw the cards across the table in a tantrum. After that, I refused to play him and he had to content himself with solitaire.

It was clear from their fur-coats the three old women were prepared to sit there all night; I left them to their pointless vigil.

I want to stress at this point; while some people may think me callous, I do not feel in any way religious. I have always found the church and its philosophy oppressive. I remember a jolly, round-faced priest who seemed to be on the best of terms with my mother, and, therefore, seemed to direct the best part of his Wednesday evening bible readings at me. Like a lot of the other kids, I was bored to tears by the catechism.

The following day, I must have been experiencing the same sense of boredom when Betty, who was standing next to me in church, shook my arm and whispered:

"Who are those old bats wearing the fur-coats?"

"One of them is the tobacconist's widow."

"She must be loaded."

"Of course, she's loaded. She's the tobacconist's widow."

"And the other two?"

I shrugged.

"I've never seen them before."

The priest, who seemed a mild man, droned on. Just when I thought he was going to wrap things up, he brought out his incense and started waving it around. I could see he was offering us – the congregation a chance to take the host. I thought I should be taking the host, but then I realised in order to take the host, one needs to go to confession. I had not been to confession for a long time, as long as I could remember.

The three old women stood up in their pews and went up the aisle towards the priest. The tobacconist's widow stuck out her tongue and the priest popped in the wafer; I was suddenly disgusted. Not only was I disgusted but glad I had not been to confession. When I turned round to tell Betty, I saw she was already making her way towards the wafer.

After what seemed like an age, the choir comprising two fat young teenagers struck up, along with the priest. They were hopeless, and quite tone deaf. It was a relief when the undertaker and his assistant came to pick up the coffin. They brought it on a trolley and we followed it down the aisle. They put it in the hearse. Although I knew it was a long drive to the crematorium, I was actually looking forward to it.

I had never been to a crematorium. Everyone here is buried in a coffin. If you are rich, they put your coffin in a mausoleum. If you are poor, they put your coffin in the cemetery wall. On the day they put my mother in a hole in the wall next to my grandfather and they blocked her up, I remember had this strange – childish notion that she was being buried alive. In contrast to the funeral, the service was mercifully short and sweet. Soft organ music played in the background as the coffin disappeared through a little curtain where I presume it was left to burn.

People here are not as a rule superstitious, unless you count superstition as the influence of the priests and their descriptions of hell. There is no doubt something of a taboo about cremation. This is the why I say now I will be sent off with my ashes scattered along with my mother's hundreds and thousands over the sea.

At the end of the ceremony, they asked me what to do with the ashes. As I had been left with no instructions, I had noticed a flowerbed full of cactus plants. The old man had never liked flowers, but I knew he liked this kind of plant. I told them to put the urn there, among the cacti.

It was dark when I dropped Betty off. When I got home, there was a man waiting for me at the entrance to the flats. Although I did not recognise him, he told me he was a friend of the old man. He offered me his condolences. We exchanged a few pleasantries; I ended up telling him about the old man's ashes buried in the flowerbed of the crematorium. He nodded – seeming to approve, though I wasn't sure because his face was pretty expressionless. Then he asked me about the old man's birds.

"You haven't sold them," he said.

"No," I said. "I didn't know there were any birds."

"Good," he said. "They should be still alive."

We went upstairs to the old man's flat. It was a long time since I had been in the flat... I opened up and switched on the light, but the bulb in the hall had gone. But I could see from the light on the landing there was a lot of junk, a familiar stand of forgotten hats and coats. On the floor was an empty birdcage.

The birds who must have heard us as we came in started up their racket; the old man's friend whose name was Bernardo disappeared down the end of the corridor; I turned on the light in the kitchen.

There was a basket of fruit on the table, with several pomegranates and two yellow melons.

I looked at the old rusting fridge where two plastic clocks in the shape of teddy bears had stopped at twelve and four respectively. A foul smell came from the bin; the cooker was full of grease, and the tiles around it smeared with eggshells. The old man never used a bowl to crack his eggs.

Bernardo came back carrying the cage with the birds. He asked me how much I wanted.

Knowing the birds were worth a bit; I said he could have the lot for five hundred. Bernardo said it was too much; I said four fifty, which is how we settled it. I threw in the empty birdcage and the bowl of fruit with the pomegranates and the two yellow melons.

I had already made my mind up I would never set foot in there again. I would send someone to clear it out in the morning. I went to bed and fell asleep in my clothes.

Was it superstition or laziness on my part? - In any case if I had not bothered to call anyone about clearing out, I realised something must have been holding me back; when the weekend came round, I found myself, at a loose end, back in the old man's flat. Since the smell from the kitchen was by now quite bad, I went into the living room and opened the shutter, and, with difficulty, because of the warped frame, the window.

The room was, as I remembered it, cluttered with furniture that had been around since my childhood. In the middle of the table, which was piled high with documents and facsimiles, there was a bowl of boiled sweets. The old man had given up smoking; it was his way of keeping temptation at bay. Behind the table was a commode with various objects – a plate depicting an Attic scene, an ornamental black elephant with real ivory tusks. Next to the commode, there was a huge, prehistoric television, which, to my surprise, still worked. Then I found myself looking round at the pictures hanging on the walls. There were several scenes from the countryside, some of the sea, a portrait of my grandfather on my father's side, who I had never met, and only knew from that portrait. He was a rather heavy-set, jowly man, who, according to legend, used to eat and fuck like a pig. Then there were the paintings done by the old man himself; the birds made out of seeds, the elephant, copied I think from the elephant on the commode. He had used red glitter for its tusks. There was also the self-portrait which included myself and my sister, Marie Angela, depicted as strange, little black dolls holding onto the hand of an Aboriginal Man painted as a skeleton.

Having always found the painting disturbing, I walked out of the room, and past the coats and the hats in the hall.

Depressed in some indefinable way, I went for a walk down on the sea front. The sea was rough; and a wind was blowing. It was bracing, and in the end I forgot my mood. I went back along the seafront and went into a bar where I saw her. It was the same woman I had seen in the bar with Giorgio.

Jazz played on the stereo behind the bar; from the expression on her face, I could see she was enjoying it.

At some point she must have looked at me; I smiled.

"Miles Davis," I said.

"This piece always makes me nostalgic about America."

I offered Giulia – for that was her name - a drink, and we started chatting about her life across the ocean. Though, for a while, I could not understand whether she liked America, or even if she still lived there and was in fact merely over here on a long holiday. It turned out Giulia was not a musician, as Giorgio had imagined, but she had two jobs. She was, or had been a teacher and was now some kind of lawyer's secretary. When I told her my friend's theory, she laughed; then we chatted about her job, which was not something I felt she particularly enjoyed doing. As it turned out, she also knew the lawyer De Santis. This in itself did not surprise me; De Santis was a well-known figure in town. She told me an amusing story about De Santis. She thanked me for the drink and left me to finish my cigarette.

I realised I had my mobile switched off.

Betty had been trying to reach me. "Where've you been? I was worried."

"I'm sorry," I said. "I've been to see a movie."

"Well," she said, "do you want to go out?"

I told her I was tired and wished to go to bed. Because she was studying, Betty did not seem to object.

The following week I received the letter from the magistrate's office informing me that the old man's flat had been confiscated and would be put up for auction. I suppose it came as something of a relief to know that the flat had been taken out of my hands. I remember I phoned and told my sister, who was of a like mind. I asked after the kids and her husband, the doctor. As we talked, I realised she had put everything behind her. There was something in her voice that was quite self-contained. I found myself thinking a little enviously on her lifestyle. She had a nice house in the suburbs with all the modern conveniences; and if I thought it was a little boring, looking after the kids and her husband, the doctor, it must have given her quiet satisfaction.

"Arturo," she said, "you will come and see us."

"Of course," I said.

In actual fact, as the winter wore on, I never got round to it. At Christmas Betty wanted to celebrate the fact that she had passed her final exam. We found a cheap flight to Sicily; I was able to take five days off work. We were lucky with the weather; when we were not on the beach, we stayed in the hotel room making love and eating watermelon that we bought from a stall on the beach. It did not feel like Christmas but summer; and we were to all intents and purposes at peace.

When we got back, it was particularly cold. Once it even snowed. It was strange to see it – because I can count on my hand the number of times I have seen it snow here. Once when I was a child and made snowballs with Giorgio's brother and we battered the girls on the way to school and got chased by the caretaker and then hauled up in front of the headmaster... I was always getting into trouble like that; things don't change.

It was the end of March. Though it often rains in March, this time we had a week of good weather. I suggested that we go and visit Edgardo and Mimi.

Perhaps I should explain; Edgardo and Mimi were old friends of my mother. When I was a child, we were always going off to visit them at the weekends. My mother seemed happy then – a feeling she must have communicated to us, because we always looked forward to it. Our trips to Edgardo and Mimi's seem bathed in idyllic light. Swimming in the sea and looking for crabs among the rocks. When it got too hot, we would get back in the car and go up the hill to Edgardo and Mimi's. The table would be set under some dried palms. We would eat baked pasta prepared by my mother or some fish dish rustled up by Mimi and sit around in the shade dosing and waiting to go back to the sea. In the middle of August, we slept in a tent in their garden and played with the children who lived in the other villas. All my adventures – including the sexual ones - began there. Edgardo and Mimi never had children. Then, when my mother died, they became like second parents to us; now they were old, we were still close. Of course, Betty knew all this, and I thought understood it; because she made no objection when I suggested we visit them. Even if I knew she preferred to go to her own villa in the country, she knew it was important to me.

The villa was about fifty kilometres out of town, tucked away in the hills above the coast...

We were early. I stopped the car by the side of the road before we arrived.

I got out and walked around. There were no poppies in the fields yet. I put on the radio and began to roll a joint… Betty took her top off and closed her eyes as the sun beat through the window. I gave her the joint. I put my hand on her thigh and let it wander up under her skirt; she was not wearing nylons but stockings; she started giggling. "Arturo," she said. "Someone will see."

"No one will see," I said, as my finger played with the elastic of her panties.

The sun was high in the sky when Edgardo's dog, Book, followed by Mimi came to meet us. We stood in the drive chatting till Edgardo came up with a bunch of wild asparagus. We sat down to lunch. The day could not have gone off better. Edgardo was a good storyteller and Mimi made a very good pasta *al forno*; I always loved her meatballs and sauce.

We had had a good day, or so I thought. And yet, in the car on the way back to town, my mood was upset by one of Betty's remarks.

Betty had happened to mention about the state of Edgardo and Mimi's house. She told me she could not go to the toilet. Although I did not say anything other than to point out that they were country people; the sense of hygiene in the country was different from that in the town, I was not just irritated but resentful. At the moment I found myself disliking Betty we nearly had an accident. We were travelling at speed on the inside lane when a car pulled out from a siding without signalling. I braked and swerved a little – straddling the outside lane. I heard Betty's scream as another car came up beside us. I took my anger out on the car by beeping at the empty road in front of us.

We spent the rest of the journey in silence; I dropped Betty at home. She called me later on my mobile, then on the landline, but each time I could not be bothered to answer. All the following week we did not speak or see each other. I have no doubt this was a factor in what happened next, even if I believe now that something – whatever it was - had been cooking in my brain since the day of the old man's funeral.

On the Saturday Toni called me up and came round in his four-wheel drive with the two girls who were to provide the entertainment.

Toni and I went way back. Though we were not good friends, we used to make a point of keeping in touch. Sometimes I would do him the odd favour with his tax for which he paid me in kind with grand gestures such as these.

Toni's girls were the kind of girls who had an eye on the main chance; Toni was only too happy to oblige with parties and events organised for politicians or local bigwigs. Although I never enquired too much, I knew, as I am sure everyone did, this put him in a position to tender for contracts with the local health department; Toni's family was in the prosthetics business.

It was not a warm night; the girls who were dressed in short skirts under their long coats laughed at Toni's jokes as he drove and flirted with them in the mirror. If obviously they had their eye on the main chance, and believed Toni could give it them, it was all very jolly in the back of the four-wheel drive.

Toni took us to a nightclub in the no-man's land on the edge of town. The final stretch was down a lane that ran down the side of the viaduct. There were potholes every five metres, and then old factory space.

A rap artist from Nottingham, England, who went by the name of Robbie Sherwood, provided the evening's entertainment. I did not like the music; while Toni and the girls went to dance up by the speakers, I stood at the back of the room and smoked my cigarette. No one seemed to care about the rules. Everyone was off their heads, or going through the motions of it.

Toni who I think was a little worried about me sent one of the girls (her name was Sabrina) to put her arms around me. He winked at me as she dragged me back onto the dance floor.

Sabrina was drunk; and I could see found it difficult to stand up in her heels. Nevertheless, she was pretty to look at and for a while I enjoyed watching her bob up and down around me until she drifted away back up to the front where Mr. Sherwood rapped over his dubs.

Someone tapped me on the shoulder. I turned round and saw it was Giulia. She smiled at me and put a drink in my hand. I took a sip and gave it back to her. For a moment we stood there listening to the music. Giulia tried to say something to me, but I couldn't hear her even when I bent my ear. Because we could not hear ourselves above the noise, Giulia took my hand and led me out towards the entrance. It was a disarming feeling – suddenly led away by this other woman; and, of course, I let myself be carried along.

"What horrible music," I said.

"Well," she said, "you have to get into it."

"Why's that?" I asked.

"Because that's the way it is now."

"You think?"

"I know… If you do get into it, then, it's not so bad."

"I must try harder," I said.

She laughed and said:

"It's not something you need to work at."

I laughed and asked if she was with someone and she said she was just thinking about leaving.

We headed out towards her car when I saw one of Toni's girls who had come out for some air. I waved to her. Either she didn't see me, or chose not to recognise me.

In the car was an open bottle of red wine, which we shared as Giulia drove. She took the circular and we headed north of the town. After a short while she turned off the main road and cut inland. "You're going to love it here," she said.

She was not wrong; we end up in a converted farmhouse with a swimming pool in the middle of a patio. The swimming pool was surrounded by busts poking out of the shrubbery. The busts, on closer inspection, appeared to be caricatures of famous politicos and celebrities.

Amused by what I saw, I told Giulia who laughed and said:

"They're not real."

"What do you mean, not real?"

"Never mind," she said. "Why don't you test the water?"

I put my hand in the pool; the water was not warm, but almost tepid. "A heated pool in this climate?"

Giulia laughed.

We entered, through the French windows, a large room full of old paintings and antique furniture to find a party of men – some chatting over brandy and cigars, others at a table where a game of poker was going on. There was a pile of notes on the table among the loose change. If the evening was for gamblers, the conversation was nothing less than urbane. When we arrived, they appeared to be talking about a novel written by a judge. One of the men sitting at the table asked Giulia for her opinion; she told him she had not read it, though she seemed to have heard of it.

They started talking about another writer called Giancarlo who was writing a detective story set in Ancient Rome.

"What's the name of the detective?"

"Aurelio."

"What a stupid name! I can think of five better names."

"For example?"

"Hack, whore…"

"Writers," said someone else, "they're either hacks or whores."

"Either that, or haunted. In this case I believe Giancarlo is a little haunted."

"Not a little hack or a little whore."

"Those," said the first speaker. "They are the best kind of writers."

I remember this snatch of conversation. At this point, a man who was sitting on the sofa with a glass of brandy picked up a magazine and brought it crashing down on the coffee table in front of him.

"Mosquitoes," he said, before returning to his seat and his brandy. For a while I studied his expression. He had the look of a man who had imbibed too much or lost everything.

When I turned round, Giulia was embroiled in a conversation with a large man wearing braces and smoking a cigar. He smiled and pulled her to him, so she was obliged to sit down on his lap.

I could not hear what they were saying. The conversation did not last long. Giulia patted him on the knee as she got up and came back over to me.

"Let's go," she said.

"What's the matter?"

"Nothing. Only he's a little piggy this evening."

"Are they all pigs?"

"No," she said, "just that one."

We got back in the car, drove back to town and parked on the seafront. A bar was open with some people, either sitting or standing outside. At one of the tables sat a transvestite and an American who Giulia seemed to know.

After a few minutes, the transvestite left us and went to talk to one of his friends inside the bar. I became curious about the American, wanting to know what he was doing in our town. It turned out he was working in a laboratory where they were developing a new tyre, one that would never wear out! I told him they would never allow him to manufacture it. He agreed it was nothing more than a pipe dream. We ordered more drinks and spent a pleasant hour chatting to the American. Sometimes the transvestite came out to chat with us before returning to chat with one of his friends. When the American told us he was tired and wanted to go home, both Giulia and I assumed he wanted to go to bed. But that was not the point; he wanted to go home to get married.

"You're not with the tranny," said Giulia.

The American laughed. "I'm far too puritanical for that."

The following day was Sunday; as I woke up, I realised I had received a text message from Betty:

Where are you, Arturo? – I miss you.

Again I did not answer, as it would have been dishonest for me to answer, since I was - at that moment in bed - in a hotel room with Giulia.

After leaving the bar with the American and his transvestite "friend", we had checked into the Sheraton and ordered breakfast – a croissant and a cappuccino. When we had finished breakfast, we had gone up to our room. Giulia started to take off her clothes in a very matter of fact way. When she was down to her underwear, she went into the bathroom and turned on the shower. I followed her in also in my underwear. She took off her bra and panties and stepped under the shower. I began to soap her down and she did the same to me until I had an erection. When we finished in the shower, we went back into the bedroom and fucked happily on the bed.

If the pleasure of this act remains etched on my mind, I felt the shadow of the winter – the cloud that the old man's death had left me under lift from me. (As if – indeed - the spunk spilled on her back, and dripping out of her bottom were proof enough of release).

When I received the message from Betty, Giulia got up from the bed and went into the bathroom to take a pee. She came back, and picked up my shirt and put it on. She sat down on the chair, and gave a sigh.

"I wonder if this is a good idea," she said.

For a while we did not speak, as if internally debating our predicament. I must have begun to mumble something about misleading her, but Giulia was quick to correct me. "If anything," she said, "I have misled myself... In actual fact, I think I am quite good at that."

At this point – and since she was involved in what she was saying – and had absently tucked her knee under her chin; the shirt fell open and she could see it had an immediate effect on me.

"I'm sorry," she said. "I shouldn't have done that." She made a point of closing her legs.

"Well," I said, "this is all very misleading."

She threw head back, laughing. The shirt fell open again.

At which point I got up and came towards her. We continued with our lovemaking, and did not check out of the hotel until the early afternoon.

Betty turned up at my office during the week. If I was a little cool towards her, she pretended – after five years I like to think I knew Betty pretty well - not to notice it. Besides, she had brought with her a Parmigiano as a peace offering.

We went back to my flat and began to prepare lunch. We took out some of the *sugo* given to us by Mimi, put it in some onion and oil, and began to cook the pasta. We put the Parmigiano in the oven to heat up. When we finished eating, Betty asked me what I thought of the Parmigiano.

I complimented her on its lightness.

"I didn't fry the aubergines," she said.

"So it was you who cooked it, not your mother?"

Betty gave me a sickly smile and asked if I wanted coffee. But I said I didn't; I wanted to go to sleep.

Did I feel guilt?

I was grateful to Betty, since she said nothing about my absences, nor my failure to answer the phone. In truth I had always admired Betty's personality; she was a woman who gave a man a certain leeway. And who was to say she was not wise? – She got what she wanted out of me – and I had the satisfaction of eliciting from her a sigh.

All this happened in the space of a few weeks in early spring, but I'm forgetting perhaps the most important element in the story.

At the beginning of the year, I had observed some workers coming and going with ladders and paint, but I did not necessarily connect their presence with my father's apartment. Periodically I would still go to check the old man's post box. One day, I noticed a letter (a gas or water bill) addressed to the new occupant, a company that went by the name of AR Holdings. This turned out to be Ivano Noviello, an out of town lawyer who sent boxes of *taralli* to a relative in the Bronx. In order to pay the mortgage, he did what most aspiring landlords do in this town and put an ad on the front door for students.

Around this time, the lift broke down. The administrator was supposed to send someone to fix it, but for whatever reason they had not come. I was coming in one evening alone when I saw Mohammed struggling with a suitcase and a rucksack on the stairs.

Mohammed, as I remember him, was a slight figure, and not particularly strong. I suppose it was an instinct, but I could see he was in trouble. The suitcase was rather heavy looking, and the rucksack – perhaps not heavy, but awkward because one of the straps had gone and there were several pairs of shoes hanging off it. When I went to help him, he must have panicked because I felt his hand gripping the suitcase even tighter. Marco, who was ahead of Mohammed on the stairs, turned round; he said something, which, of course, I did not understand. Mohammed's hand seemed to relax, and I was able to help him up the stairs with the suitcase.

Although we fought shy of actual conversation, we started greeting each other on the stairs. Marco was naturally less shy than Mohammed; he always smiled when he saw us; and if I did not think about it very consciously, I remember Betty would smile back.

No doubt there was something about Marco. He seemed pretty open and friendly. Not as I would imagine a Muslim. Mohammed, on the other hand, seemed to conform to all the stereotypes one hears. – He had dark features; he was silent, almost brooding and surly. Although I did not fully realise at the time, he understood very little of our language. Marco, however, spoke it quite well – but with an accent. In fact, it seemed in the short time he'd been in the town he'd picked up some dialect and expressions. I remember once – I happened to be stepping into Giulia's car - he called to me in the street: "How's it going, boss?" He actually used the word "capo", which to my ears sounded funny since the sort of thing a worker says to his supervisor.

It was my day-off I recall. After the government cutbacks, if you did over-time, you would not necessarily get paid, but you could take time off. – My boss was only happy to oblige. It was lunchtime; Betty and I had been to the market, and we'd bought some fish when we met Mohammed and Marco coming back from the medical faculty. Marco called to me: "Good morning, capo", and to Betty, "Good morning, "Signora". Of course, I think he meant to say "Signorina". – It was Betty, I think, who suggested it. - Why not invite them to lunch?

Although I think we were both curious about them, we tried not to show it.

We cooked them a proper meal with starters (aubergines in garlic and oil). The first course was rigatoni with tomato sauce. The tomatoes were from Edgardo's garden, and the basil from my balcony. The sea bream was fresh, not farmed, and stuffed with parsley and garlic, again from Edgardo's garden. We put water and wine on the table, which of course they did not touch. I cannot say if they really appreciated it, but they were exceptionally polite. Although Mohammed refused the hard ricotta cheese that you grate onto the pasta, I think that he was allergic to cheese.

If the conversation was on the awkward side of stilted, I could see Marco made a big effort. Mohammed, on the other hand, said very little. When he spoke, we did not always understand him; I am sure that influenced our attitude. Afterwards Betty and I joked because at that time the Americans were in Afghanistan looking for Bin Laden. It was nothing personal – just a little private joke. I told Giorgio at work; Giorgio came up with a much better joke, which is why we started calling them the Trainee Doctors of Death. Of course, this had no bearing on reality; Mohammed and Marco were just young lads, fish out of water.

As a rule, and for obvious reasons, Julia would not ring me. If I didn't answer by the third ring, she knew I was with Betty and would hang up. I actually had 3 numbers for Julia all under different names. If Betty asked me who they were, I would refer to them vaguely as someone at work, or a friend of Toni. – I have often asked myself why we went along with all this. – It was quite mad – destined to go pear-shaped. But we kept it up for the best part of three months between hotels and Julia's flat (even if, again for obvious reasons, we were not comfortable there). A peculiarity of these arrangements was that we took it in turns to pay the bill; Julia would insist on that. In that way she was very upright and English, though not I would say in bed.

I don't want to give the impression that we were always thinking about making love or contriving to bring it about. It was the spring, after all. Sometimes, in the afternoons, except Tuesdays and Thursdays when I was in the office, we made our way down the coast to have coffee or pistachio – Julia's favourite - ice cream. Or we would catch the first show at the old cinema on Corso Sonnino - holding hands, like two teenagers, in the back row. Or we would meet at the tower on the beach at San

Vito - clambering over the rocks until we found a spot far away from prying eyes. These simple little pleasures no doubt added to the illicit ones!

Once and only once, I recall Julia turning up at my flat; she was wearing a business suit, and she had a briefcase in her hand. She told me she had been to court... By this time, I knew, though the subject was never broached between us, she was still involved with Achille Lombardo. I remember she put her briefcase down on the kitchen table and walked around it slowly as if she was admiring it. – Really there is nothing special about my kitchen. Then she turned to me and told me she would like to see the bedroom. We never in fact made it to the bedroom. As we were improvising over the kitchen table, the doorbell rang. Julia said afterwards, I ran around like Lino Banfi in a "Carry On", pulling up my trousers and struggling with my belt. - It was Marco who'd come down for a chat. - This was just after Mohammed had gone back home to deal with family problems even if the joke (mine and Betty's) was he'd gone back to plan some terrorist activity. - Well, I couldn't exactly invite him in. The kitchen in my flat is just off the hall, and Julia didn't have her underwear on.

If he understood what was going on – and I thought about it a lot afterwards, he didn't say anything. I told him to come back later. Betty was coming round that evening for something to eat, and afterwards we were going to go out... Did he want to come?

In turning to the events of that weekend, I had sent Julia a message to meet at the bookshop in Via M-; we often met at the bar there, before we went off one of our jaunts. I had taken up my usual place in the window. I was looking out onto the street when I saw Julia coming out of an office across the road. With her was Achille Lombardo. As I was watching them, they stopped outside the entrance; Achille Lombardo bent down and kissed Julia on the lips. If I couldn't see Julia's face because she had her back to me, I must have perceived something in her attitude - the tilt of her neck, the cascade of her hair. It seemed to me not just a peck on the cheek, but a full embrace – one of significant intimacy. I was taken aback. It was as if, in that moment, I realised the truth of the situation – that there was perhaps more to their marriage than I had imagined. Nevertheless, all these thoughts I kept to myself when

Julia came up to me in the bookshop coffee bar and kissed me on the cheek. "Have you missed me?" she said in English.

"You know I missed you," I said.

She smiled and squeezed my hand.

We drove along the seafront with the windows down – then along the coast road up past the abandoned villas and ramshackle whorehouses. Where the road cuts in land between the main road and the olive fields and vineyards, I put on some music.

The *complanare* was all but empty. I know this stretch of road very well. As we passed the Tamoil garage with its prehistoric pumps, and came up over the hill that brings you down towards the sea, I began to drive in time to the music. Julia started laughing. She put her hand on my leg, and started caressing me until we were both laughing.

It was a perfect day with not a cloud in sight. I want to impress on you the view from that stretch of coast with the fields of prickly pears and untilled land that tumbles down towards the rock beaches and inlets. A couple of years ago, they started blocking access to the sea with their so-called "private roads", which are actually against the law. It was down one of these roads that I took the car. We parked under some trees, took the beach bag with our towels out of the boot and walked down to the sea.

The sea was flat and calm; there was not a boat on the horizon.

We picked our way among the rocks until we came to an inlet. We put down our towels and stripped off. We were both naked as we jumped in the water. The sea had not yet warmed up, and the water was still cold. We paddled around flapping our arms until we got warm. Because we didn't really get warm, even by splashing about, we got out and lay back in the sun, drying ourselves. Then we started touching and caressing each other. If there was no one about, we pulled the towels around us for modesty's sake. I remember Julia had her back turned slightly from me because I was entering her from behind. I felt myself coming before she was ready to come. I was still inside her; my cock was no longer hard. How can I explain? Trying my best to make her come, I felt helpless. - Not at my own sexual performance which can be as varied as the weather. If I felt helpless, it was helplessness of another kind. - As though I was losing Julia, and not just to Achille Lombardo's money.

I had arranged with Betty to go to Toni's party. We always enjoyed Toni's parties. Toni had a flair for organisation, and his parties were rightly famous. People would come from all over just to be at one of his "masseria" country dos. Betty wanted to invite Marco; I was happy to go along with her idea. As I have said, we both liked Marco. He was good company; I was – I suppose – pleased that Betty had someone she wanted to bring along. By now, you will appreciate my life was becoming more than just a little complicated. My only regret, of course, was that I could not bring Julia. I remember I sent her a message, but for some reason she did not answer… I was just beginning to wonder why she hadn't as we drove to the party; the idea entered my head, as it had done when I had seen her with Achille Lombardo, and later at the beach when we made love that she was getting ready to leave me.

Music blared out from the back of the stone-floored room. You could not see the decks – only the floppy hat of the DJ bobbing up and down to the sound of drum and bass. Betty took Marco's hand and dragged him into the room.

I was thirsty and wanted a drink. Set out on a trestle table inside the room was a bowl of fruity-looking punch that did not appeal to me. I went to get a beer from a large ice bucket that was standing in the entrance. A bottle-opener hung on a piece of string at the side.

I turned round and saw Marco dancing. I was surprised; in some prejudiced way, I did not have Marco down as a dancer. As I watched him moving round Betty, I saw he was actually quite good, twisting and turning his body. – Betty was leaning into him with a smile on her face. At that moment Toni came up to me and we started talking. Because we could not hear ourselves think, above the noise, we went outside.

Some friends came up to Toni; they slapped hands in that ritual way they have on these occasions of forcing joy. They passed us and walked on towards the music, while we went and stood among the cars parked in the field; I took out a cigarette; Toni took a rolled joint from his top pocket. We passed the cigarette and the joint back and forth.

"Well, what do you reckon?" said Toni.

As he spoke, the lights from the masseria behind us went off, along with the music.

It has always amazed me, the patience of midnight revellers. It took them a good half an hour to get the lights and the music back on. By that time, the punch was more fruit than alcohol, and there was more ice than beer in the bucket. But when the lights came back on, everyone, excluding myself, went dance crazy. In the meantime, I had been trying to get hold of Julia. I tried all three numbers I had for her, but whatever number I chose Julia did not answer. I was on the point of giving up when someone picked up the phone. It wasn't Julia I heard but a man's heavy breathing...

I lost track of time. I remember asking Marco where Betty had got to. He smiled and shrugged. I went outside looking for her among the vines. I found her sitting on a bench at the end of a path. "*Tutt' a posto?*" I said. "Are you all right?"

Betty did not answer.

After a while, I said:

"Are you going to come and dance?"

I took her hand but she pulled it away. She told me to leave her alone.

Some more beers had turned up from somewhere. I got steadily drunk. From time to time, I would see Betty dancing with Marco. There was, it seemed, nothing I could do about it except get drunker than I already was.

The party broke up around four o'clock in the morning. We did not drive back to town; instead, we went to Betty's family villa, so handily placed down the road. In fact, it was often a useful stopover for us as we made our way from one party to another in the early summer months before her parents moved there for the holidays.

I went to bed with a hangover. When I woke up the following day, Betty and Marco were already awake and making breakfast. When they saw me, I thought, although it could have been my paranoia, they seemed to stop talking. But I pretended not to notice and drank my coffee. We played a polite game at the breakfast table. Marco smiled his amiable smile. Betty, he said, had told him all about the beach and he was looking forward to it. "*Non vedo l'ora,*" he said, trying out a new expression.

"In that case," I said, "you will know about the Finger."

Marco looked at Betty.

"He means the rock," she said, "where all the macho boys go diving."

I told him it had other more vulgar names.

Marco smiled. He said he would like to try it. Then he told us about a beach back at home, where, if I understood him, there was a similar kind of rock.

"How high up is it?" I asked.

"Well, you know," he said, raising his eyes heavenwards. Then he pulled one of his funny faces.

I laughed and so did Betty.

When we arrived at the beach, it must have been about eleven o'clock. I was dying to get into the water and clear my head. I could have just splashed my head and jumped in, but after the conversation with Marco at the breakfast table, I thought we should do it the proper way. If Marco had not wanted to oblige me, I would not have blamed him. As it was, he did not want to disoblige me. And perhaps, although I'm guessing, he wanted to impress Betty, because she did not want him to go. She said it could be dangerous if you did not know what you were doing. Marco did not seem to mind; in fact, he said it was okay, he wanted to do it. It would be fun. – Those are the words I remember: "it would be fun."

We started climbing up the side of the Finger. While it is not exactly a "walk in the park", it is also quite safe, since there are plenty of places to put your feet, even with flip-flops. When you reach the top, there is a kind of platform; I suppose it is a little like being at the top of an Olympic diving board, only a little higher; someone once told me by about five metres or so. The only snag is that when you jump, or dive – though I would not recommend a "novice" to dive, there are one or two rocks that jut out; in that case you must make sure you jump or dive clear. If you don't, you can catch your foot. I remember when we reached the top, and we stood on the platform, I took Marco to the edge, and showed him the rocks. I think it was quite clear in my mind that I had to make him aware of the danger.

Now I come to the point where I cannot honestly remember. – Has my mind blanked what happened out of shock, or something more terrible? –The police say they have their witnesses. Later, I found out from the report the name of the witnesses was one Rodriguez D.

Was it I wonder the same Rodriguez D with whom I was at school? – Rodriguez D and unnamed others say that when Marco jumped I pushed him. This is why he caught himself on the rocks and went tumbling to his death. Even if in some mad way, and given my state of mind, I might have had reason, I cannot imagine doing this. – I cannot believe that I had become so unhinged and bitter, even if I thought I was losing them both – both Julia and Betty… it just would not have made any sense.

The last thing I remember I was in the water, and coming up for air. As I did, I remember looking round for Marco and not being able to see him, I swam around until it occurred to me that I had better head back towards the beach

In the casino of the cruiser a billet was handed to me on a silver tray. When I found Q's cabin, I realised I was drowning in bathwater.

***

The Permesso

The bus took her up past the cemetery and through the industrial estate. The road was full of potholes and when the bus went over the bumps she winced. The pain in her stomach had returned.

Then they hit the wasteland. Among the abandoned fields was an old villa that must have been important once, but now the walls were crumbling and the frames had been stolen from the windows. From the top of the lama, she saw the sea, which was flat. A haze hung around a pair of fishing smacks on the water.

The bus passed through a quarter with ugly high-rise blocks made of cheap materials, and low-cost supermarkets, built over thirty years ago during the boom.

At the end of the line, she got off the bus with some school children in blue pinafores. She watched as they crossed the road by the traffic lights; she couldn't see their school.

Across the road from the prison was a row of shops, including a bar and tobacconist's. By the side of the road, she noticed was a man with a withered arm who was selling watermelons from a three-wheeler.

At the gates of the prison the guard asked to see her papers; she showed her identity-card.

The guard told her she could not enter; she needed a permesso.

She asked if she could speak to his superior.

The young Signora was made to wait, as the guard allowed the other visitors to enter.

An old woman passed her with a bucket of figs. – "This is for the Captain," she said, putting the bucket down on the table.

The Guard nodded. She handed a smaller bag to the guard.

The guard went away and came back a while later. With him was another older guard, who led her into a back office.

On the desk was an ashtray of cigarette butts and a glass bottle of Monticchio water. A peaked cap resting on a pile of documents.

Above the desk was a signed photo of the local football team. Their haircuts were too long and their shorts too short to be the current team. A postcard icon of a saint was tucked into the cheap wooden frame. Manila files and facsimiles were piled on top of two battered filing cabinets.

The second guard turned out to be as inflexible as the first. "You need a permesso," he said. "If you don't have permesso, we can't do anything."

"Where can I get a permesso?"

"From the Captain."

"I would like to speak to the Captain."

The guard shrugged. The Captain, he said, was busy with other things.

Leaving the prison, she met the old woman carrying her empty bucket. As they walked to the bus stop, the old woman struggled on rickety legs, muttering to herself.

They got on the bus. The old woman turned to the young Signora and said something, but she did not understand. The old woman was speaking in dialect.

Returning to the flat, she collapsed on the bed and fell asleep. When she awoke, her mobile was ringing in the dark.

By the time she picked it up, the caller had rung off. She lay with the sheet wrapped round her.

Her mobile rang again; she picked it up on the second ring.

The voice on the other end was distant. "I can't hear you," she said. "The line comes and goes."

"Now," he said, "can you hear me?"

"Yes," she said.

"What are you doing?" he asked.

"Sleeping," she said.

His voice was again distant.

"The line's still bad," she said.

"Is that better?"

"Yes, I can hear you now. What do you want?"

The man on the end of the line did not speak for a while. Finally, he said, "I'll be out of town for a few days."

"Where are you?"

But she did not his reply; the line went dead. She put the mobile down on the bed and went out onto balcony to smoke a cigarette.

A film of sand lay on the bus windows. A pool of sweat ran down into the small of her back as she stepped off the bus behind the school children in blue pinafores.

At the gates of the prison, she was again made to wait. Finally, the guard led her into the back office. She looked down and saw the peaked cap still lying on the pile of documents.

The man sitting at the desk was smoking a cigarette. He looked up, registering her presence, and turned to the guard.

"Have you got the time sheet?"

"Yes, Captain."

The Guard handed over a paper. "Is there anything else, Captain?"

The Captain did not say anything; the guard turned to go.

The Captain put his cigarette down in the ashtray.

The Captain, she noted, was wearing a watch - a chunky and fashionably expensive timepiece with a dial.

The Captain sat studying his documents; he put them down on the table and looked at her. When he spoke, she was surprised to hear him use the archaic "voi" - not the "lei" form of address.

The young Signora began to explain the purpose of her visit. As the Captain listened, he picked up his cigarette and drew on it. For a while, he seemed to consider her request. When he spoke again, however, the young Signora understood that he had not heard her. Instead, he spoke about rules and regulations, and the importance of *permessi*. "This may sound a strange question," he said with scrupulous politeness. "Are you not from around here?"

No, she said, as a matter of fact, she wasn't.

"I thought as much," he said.

Though he took pains to compliment her, he had detected a northern cadence in the young Signora's accent. "I assume you are from the north? – Then, you would not understand how we do things here."

"We are particularly attached to the rules," he said. "If we don't adhere to the rules and regulations, chaos ensues."

He made a gesture as if chaos had been unleashed. "I hope I have explained myself," he said.

She nodded and thanked him for taking the trouble to speak to her.

Before she left the room, the Captain called to her. "I am sorry you have wasted your time."

When she got back to the flat, she stripped off her clothes and stood under the shower. The cold tap ran warm before it ran cold.

Hardly bothering to dry herself off, she sat in her underwear, watching the TV.

She held her stomach, but the pain would not go away.

Later, getting up the courage to go out, she walked down the street towards the sea. It was early evening, and she met a group of boys playing football in the strips of their favourite players. She crossed the road to avoid them and crossed back again as she passed them.

The chemist gave the young Signora a confection of pills. "You should go to the hospital," she said. "Either that, or you should see your doctor."

The young Signora nodded.

In the night, at the point of reckoning, she woke up sweating and calling out her lover's name. She got up; went and sat on the toilet; she held her stomach.

Before she left the flat, she took another pill.

When she got off the bus, there was nowhere to hide from the sun and the heat.

The young Signora entered the bar opposite the gates of the prison. The air was cool and crisp from the air conditioning.

The barman asked her what she wanted. Though she did not want anything, she ordered a lemon *granita* and sat down at a table.

When the Captain came in, he went over to the bar and ordered a coffee. He turned round and gave her a smile.

The barman placed his coffee on the counter. The Captain picked it up and took a sip.

He continued to smile at her.

When he finished his coffee, he walked over to her table and asked if she minded if he sat down.

The seat was almost too small for him. He turned the chair outwards so he could spread his legs.

As he continued to look at her, without speaking, she looked down at his watch.

The Captain, who noted this, smiled. "It's water-resistant", he said, "up to thirty metres."

He began to tell her about his fishing exploits. Down on the coast, he went with his gun hunting for bass and bream. "They're not easy to catch," he said. "We've fished these waters to death. The funny thing is we don't care… We will go on fishing them to death."

The idea seemed to lend a tragic expression to his face. She looked down at his watch.

"I don't know if we have much time," he said.

When he got up, she followed him out.

The hotel was on the second floor of a three-storey apartment block. The shutters were down in the room, but the sun was peeking through the slats at the bottom.

The bed had a simple wooden board; there was a table with an ashtray and a couple of chairs with wicker seats. Hanging on the wall was a cherub with some dried flowers.

The Captain took his cigarettes out of his pocket. He put them down on the table, beside the ashtray. He took off his watch. Then he took off his jacket and hung it over the back of one of the chairs.

She sat on the edge of the bed and unbuttoned her dress. She let it slip to the floor.

When the Captain had finished, he got up and sat at the table smoking a cigarette.

He put his jacket back on and left the room.

The following day, arriving at the gates of the prison, the young Signora asked to see the Captain; the guard told her the Captain was not on duty.

"I have come to see one of the prisoners," she said. "I am sure the Captain has left me the permesso."

The guard disappeared into the back office.

After a while, he returned.

"I am sorry, Signora," he said. "You do not have the permesso.

It is the stranger in you to whom I am now making this – I admit – clumsy appeal.

***

Stranger on the Shore

The businessman Achille Lombardo had taken his wife on an all-expense paid trip to Switzerland. After their meal with esteemed colleagues and friends, she made her excuses and left him in the lobby. About fifteen minutes later, he followed her up to their room.

He sat down at a chair beside the bed. She continued to ignore him; he picked up a magazine from the bedside table.

After a while he put the magazine back down on the bedside table. He turned to her and said:

"Forgive me, my darling. What is it you wish me to do?"

"What is it I wish?" she said, repeating the question rather as if it was a rhetorical device deployed by a brittle heroine in an unremarkable play. "I wish you to leave."

Not long after this Achille Lombardo's marriage broke up. He and his wife separated, though they did not divorce.

Achille Lombardo moved into the room at the back of his office. It was a simple room with no flowers and no TV. Achille Lombardo brought his laptop and consoled himself by watching old movies he hadn't seen in decades. He sat down to write his autobiography, but realised after a while that he was writing fiction and so he gave up.

Achille Lombardo threw himself into his work and partied with old university friends who he thought were as awkward and bitter as he. A while passed. Achille Lombardo was still living in the room where he had no TV and barely slept. He woke up one day with palpitations. He went to see an esteemed cardiologist, Dr Carducci. When he arrived in the surgery, the cardiologist Dr Carducci was chatting with another esteemed colleague who he referred to – somewhat facetiously – as the neurologist Doctor Tom-Tom. While he thought it was not very professional, Achille Lombardo did not say anything.

"What appears to be the matter, dear fellow?"

Describing his symptoms, Achille Lombardo complained of stomach cramps, bad dreams and sleepless nights.

Dr Carducci took his blood pressure, which did not tally with Achille Lombardo's own heart-felt reading. His heart beat was as steady as that of a long-distance runner Etc.

Esteemed colleagues scratched their heads. There appeared to be nothing wrong with Achille Lombardo, suffice it to say he had lost ten kilos in the space of a few months and slimmed down to the size he was when he was about twenty-one.

At the end of the visit, they proscribed some pills.

Achille Lombardo was worried. Esteemed colleagues looked to reassure him. Really, they soothed, it's little more than a placebo… He must learn to relax. Take a holiday.

Thus, on the advice of esteemed colleagues, Achille Lombardo went south, and rented a small villa on the beach. It was the middle of September, and the weather was still fine. The forecast was going to be good for the next two weeks. Achille Lombardo imagined paddling in the sea and idling in his shorts and sandals in the sun.

The following day, while Achille Lombardo was having his breakfast on the veranda, a stray dog turned up at the villa. Achille Lombardo wasn't feeling hungry so he gave the dog some biscuits. He went for a walk along the beach. The dog followed him. Hey, where do you think you are going, you pesky mongrel?

The dog followed him back to the villa. Realising he had been adopted; Achille Lombardo took the dog to the vet. The vet was reassuring. The dog was as fit as a fiddle. Achille Lombardo took the dog back to the villa. They went for a walk on the beach. The beach was long and sandy and wide and flat with some dunes at the back. Both patient and dog liked to walk there and play with the sand and the seaweed on the shore.

The patient liked to take photos. Although he had never been a professional photographer, in another life he thought it would have been just the job for him. He began – under the watchful eye of his new-found friend - to take interest in the objects washed up on the shore: its flotsam and jetsam…

Two days ago, for example, he took a photo of a blue bucket. The blue bucket did not have a handle. It was sticking out of the sand, as the sea lapped around it.

Up by the dunes, yesterday, he found an empty coke can between two sticks bleached by the sun…Then, unexpectedly, he came across one of a pair of orange flip-flops. Though I cannot explain why Achille Lombardo did not take a photo; when he got back to the villa he was overcome with a profound sort of depression.

In the late afternoon, when the dog came to wake him, he did not want to get out of bed, any more than he wanted to go back to the long wide beach. No amount of tail wagging or leash shaking on the dog's part could persuade him otherwise. The patient Achille Lombardo was patently not in the mood.

Achille Lombardo fell back to sleep; he began to dream he was back on the beach. Not the beach described here which is not dissimilar to the beaches I remember from my childhood... i.e. long and empty, but not unwelcoming.

The beach in Achille Lombardo's dream is quite different. It is not my beach but one which I also know.

This beach, Achille Lombardo's beach is quite inaccessible to traffic. One side of the cliff has fallen in, which is why it is risky to run a vehicle there. Beyond this point, there are a series of little coves where students, young couples and solitary bathers like to go.

In one of the coves there is a rock island. On the small sandy part of the beach Achille Lombardo can see a solitary bather. When the beach is crowded (by this I mean there is a handful of people, for example, students in Bermuda shorts sharing beers and joints, old men in scruffy shorts and the odd fisherman), the bather often swims out to the rock island.

In Achille Lombardo's dream, everything happens as it normally does. The bather swims out to the rock-island and lies there as is her wont to sunbathe with her top off...

It is a such a peaceful scene. Indeed, we can all breathe in its calm serene!

The black clouds creep up on her. He tells it to me like that. "Doctor," he says, "the black clouds creep up on her. The air is suddenly very cold, and the sea around her is very still."

Ordinarily (Achille Lombardo can testify to this) she is a good swimmer, since she has been in the school team, but the current is strong. The current pulls her hither and thither. As the current pulls her hither and thither, the patient dreamer finds himself sinking down and down with her till he wakes up, sweating.

Achille Lombardo gets up and goes into the kitchen to get himself a glass of water. He looks round for his new friend, but he cannot see the dog. He walks out onto the veranda.

When, in the distance upon the shore, he sees the stranger walking with the dog at her side, he tells me he makes a solemn vow.

"Doctor, will I ever be able to exorcise the dream?"

Although you are in trouble and everyone is against you, I want you to know that I am, exclusively, on your side.- On Behalf of the Good Egg

***

The Recital

Outside the lawyer's office a man was kneeling on the pavement, with his arms above his head holding a plastic cup. Rodriguez fumbled in his pocket, put fifty cents into the plastic cup and rang the bell.

There was a queue of people waiting to see the lawyer. In their hands they held facsimiles and manila envelopes.

Rodriguez sat down on one of the vacant chairs and waited listening to the conversations around him dictated by facsimiles and manila envelopes.

By the time Rodriguez entered the lawyer's office it was getting towards dinner and all the lawyer's clients had gone home.

The lawyer looked up from his papers and peered at Rodriguez across his desk. "Diego," he said, "perhaps you have been wondering why I have summoned you here. After all, we have not been in contact for a number of years."

As the lawyer explained what was required of him, Rodriguez listened, not quite believing his ears.

Although never quite of the top draw, Rodriguez had been an accomplished enough musician. He had played at one time for the San Carlo before being persuaded that there was a *poltrona*, or nice comfy chair of a position waiting for him in the local orchestra. An embarrassing series of incidents involving a several glasses of wine and the odd cheroot cigar had precipitated his decline. If now he struggled to make ends meet, and they rarely called him for the orchestra, he knew it was nothing personal, unless of course you considered it personal being passed over for a place-man. Now Rodriguez got by playing weddings and parties. He played on the streets during festivals, but he was tired of that kind of work and wanted to stop.

The lawyer, astute fellow, must have picked up on this.

"Of course, you will be well compensated."

Rodriguez did not ask him how much. The lawyer named the figure; Rodriguez was tempted to whistle.

Pushing a piece of paper across the table where a map had been drawn, the lawyer explained how to get to the rendezvous point.

"The recital is tomorrow evening, which I appreciate does not give you much time."

Rodriguez was all ready to make a quip when the lawyer took out a gold fountain pen from his pocket and asked for his bank details. "Your fee," he said, "will be paid into your account after the recital."

Rodriguez got up to go.

"A matter of curiosity… How did your client hear of me?"

The lawyer smiled.

"It was a restaurant… about six months ago."

Rodriguez thought hard but he had no firm recollection of a restaurant assignation. Yet, in his mind's eye, he had a picture of a young couple. The girl was not particularly pretty, but he remembered her expression of delight when her fiancé produced the ring from a little blue box. The thought of it almost reduced him to tears.

It was getting dark when Rodriquez arrived at the rendezvous point. They drove for about thirty minutes before turning off the main road.

The road twisted and turned for a further fifteen or twenty minutes until they arrived at the gates of the castle. Rodriguez knew it was a castle because he put his hand out to steady himself and he felt the damp stone wall.

They led him up some stairs to what might have been a mezzanine floor and helped him get to his seat. Rodriguez got out his violin and, though he could not see anything through his blindfold, began to tune his instrument.

On his left he made out the shape of a stone balcony. Below him he heard voices, murmured conversations. He tried to imagine the guests. Who they might be? - Local politicians, dignitaries, policemen? – But before his imagination took a paranoid turn, the voices subsided.

In the silence, Rodriquez took up his violin and began to draw his bow.

As he did, he heard the voice of the singer from across the way. The voice had a strange, unsettling effect;

Rodriguez had to fight to maintain his bow and stop himself from fainting.

Three days later, Rodriguez was sitting at a table in the *mensa* in the old town when, behind him in the canteen, he heard the voice again.

"What has happened to him?" said a nun.

"I think he's had a heart attack."

"Well, don't just stand there! Call the ambulance!"

Poor Diego! Never got his just desserts. The money he made from the recital went to the nuns and the mensa. His death did not even make a footnote in the Gazette.

On Furlough

The man could not remember anything about his life except that he was once a cook in South Africa. The hospital eventually traced his brother who came to see him. His brother shakes him by the hand, gives him thirty Euros, then says goodbye. (From Doctor Tom Tom's case studies in Amnesia)

When Arturo left the restaurant, the violinist was still playing. Walking out along the main drag towards the Palazzo del Governo, he came across some workers huddled around a fire in the municipal car park. From a supermarket trolley, they had erected a banner that read:

The Government is a dictatorship of the proletariat.

Across the road, on the steps of the provincial theatre, stood a squad of police officers. - Between the two opposing camps what remained of a kitchen unit, the metal rim that once sealed its plastic top uncoiling across the road. It seemed to Arturo quite absurd – the squad or small army of police officers watching, at a distance, and from the safety of the theatre steps, to see whether the striking workers would throw another childish fit and hurl their banner with its anachronistic and indeed contradictory message.

After they discharged him from the hospital, Arturo had not gone back to work. The tax office owed him a week's holiday. With time on his hands, however, he did not feel like doing anything except idling in the flat and watching TV. It surprised him when he received the phone call from his ex. For a while, they behaved like two mice treading around broken eggs until something in him snapped.

"It feels like you are still judging me."

"I'm not judging you, Arturo. Let's face it. We both behaved badly. But don't you think it's time you stopped living in the past?"

When the phone rang again, Arturo wasn't going to answer; then changed his mind. It was his sister wondering how he was getting on. "I'm just fine," he said.

"No, you're not."

"Yes, I am. How are the kids?"

"Why don't you speak to Corrado?"

His nephew, who was learning the piano, hummed the tune to jingle bells down the phone… His sister tried to make him promise to visit. Arturo did not promise anything; instead, he bought some almond cakes and a bouquet of flowers and got in his car.

Arturo drove along the coast road for about half an hour before turning inland towards the hills that lay back from the sea. Then, seemingly without paying attention, he turned away from the hills and drove down an increasingly narrow lane until he arrived at an old, flecked white gate. He got out of the car, bearing his gifts.

The old man came out to meet him; he was hanging onto his walking stick.

They embraced. "*Vecchio.*"

"*Giovane.*"

The old man smiled and patted him on the back.

The old man's wife had cooked a simple tomato sauce. For the "second", she had baked artichokes with breadcrumbs and mozzarella. A neighbour had given the old man a bottle of Primitivo. "It's got a nice full body," he said. "Like that of a Signora who's been working the fields all her life."

They ate their meal without saying much, except in sly allusions to old times. From time to time, they joked, as they used to, about local affairs as seen through a thin veil of tears.

The conversation took a philosophical turn. The old man declared he did not understand anything anymore and would be glad when he was gone.

His wife told him to stop talking nonsense.

The old man smiled as if he knew she was right. "If I come back again," he said, "I would like it to be as a cricket."

"Why is that?" their guest asked.

"Isn't it obvious?" said the old man. "They are fast and hop round."

"Well done," said his wife. "They get caught in your hand and used for bate."

"Woman," he said, "what do you know about fishing?"

The old woman set the coffee on the table. They drank their coffees with the almond cakes and chewed the fat until it was time for the old man's rest.

Arturo helped the old woman put away the things. When they had finished, he said he would go outside for a walk.

The old woman nodded.

"You better take your jacket," she said. "It gets cold about now."

Arturo slipped over the fence at the back of the house and cut across a wasteland onto a path that took him through a succession of small, canopied vineyards.

In the sky above him was a bank of cloud that began to make faces and disconcert him. As if, in that bank of cloud, he could discern the faces of the old gods that may still watch over us, he drew his jacket round him and hurried along the path between the fields.

The fields he passed ran uphill in tiers. If Arturo knew them well, it seemed he did not pay much attention to where he was going until, pulled out of his reverie, he came to a field full of spring flowers and long grass.

There, ahead of him was a copse. Approaching the copse, he saw the heads of some asparagus sprouting from the undergrowth. A shudder went down his back; Arturo began to weep.

How long did he lie on the ground – at the mercy of grief? – The field was wet and his clothes began to feel damp. In the end, he got up and went into the copse to pick the asparagus.

After this, he walked the length of a drystone wall, picking the asparagus in the cracks. Then he scoured the prickly pears in the field behind and picked the asparagus with great juicy heads that sprouted in their shadows. He climbed up onto an old stone dome roof and picked the asparagus among the brambles. Then he walked along the wall of a wet field and picked the asparagus from among the loose stones as dogs barked at him across the wasteland. When he had a big bundle in his hands, he tied them together with a leaf of grass and returned to the house.

The old couple was in the kitchen. "Look," said the old woman, "he's picked quite a bunch."

Arturo put the bundle of asparagus down on the table.

"*Vecchio*," said the old woman. "Don't just sit there gloating... Go fetch the eggs."

Born in Poole, Dorset, in 1965, Sedley Proctor grew up in London and was educated in Winchester and Nottingham. He lived and worked as a teacher and translator in Southern Italy from the mid-nineties until 2013 when he returned to Britain. Apart from his own books, he writes under the aliases F.N. Frites and M.T. Sands.

ACKNOWLEDGEMENTS

The cover of this book has been designed with a derivative of an I-stock photo, woman on a beach, under a standard royalty free license. The Harlequin, or *Jolly Nero* is a derivative of a digital photo donated by Trocche 100 to the public domain.

The Half Days

By Sedley Proctor

Ex-pat adventure in Southern Italy

Young, English teacher, Julia arrives in a vibrant Southern Italian city where she takes up with happy-go-lucky street seller, Cofi. When Cofi is caught up in a smuggling ring, the question of her own future arises. But as the half days stretch into the summer nights, the future is forgotten in a round of carnival pleasures.

Ten Naughty Stories

By M T Sands

"A luminous bit of prose delicately piled on prose platters"

Jay Parini

M.T. Sands grew up in southern England. She ran away from school when she was sixteen and lost her virtue in a field in Burgundy, under the vines of Clos de Tart, to a mystical and long-haired young German who claimed to be able to divine the kabbalah from a rather weathered notebook which had H. H. inscribed in fading, gold leaf on the cover. For several days she followed him on her bicycle until she ate some Pierre che Rire cheese and realized she was being an absolute fool. Thereafter her career began.

ALSO AVAILABLE FROM LEOPARD

CHILDREN'S FICTION

***

It was a matter of some urgency: a wolf was loose in the woods. And being loose in the woods, he could get into the garden.

"Whatever you do," said Dad. "Don't go out the gate. You don't want the wolf to eat you."

Laila went out the door, but the wolf was already in the garden.

"There you are!" he cried. "I was wondering where you got to."

"What are you doing here?" she cried. "This is my garden."

"Well," said the wolf, "you're not in your garden. You're in my garden now."

***

The Wolf Garden

By F. M. Frites

A Totally, Completely and Utterly Bodacious Adventure with Unicorns and Gnomes

Dreamy tomboy, Laila meets Cyril, a rebellious gnome and passes through a charmed gate into the Wolf Garden. Here, she does battle with the shape-shifter Smarm and his army of wolves. When Smarm captures her gnome friends and steals the magic strawbs, Laila and Cyril help the Mistress Dido win them back.